**Warrior Queen – Rani**



Bikramī 2078

Nanakshāhī 552

This book is an English adaptation of the 1953 Panjabi novel by Giani Trilok Singh. 

**ISBN 978-1-8381437-2-5**

Printed in the UK by KhalisHouse Publishing.

**More info:**

www.KhalisHouse.com

info@KhalisHouse.com

**Find us on:**

Instagram/KhalisHouse

Twitter/KhalisHouse

This book is dedicated to Sarohi Kaur.

Sarohi, my child, may you find strength and inspiration from the bold and daring actions of the mighty warrior queens of Panjab.

# WARRIOR QUEEN
# RANI SADA KAUR

# 1.

The city of Batala, which today lies in the modern-day District of Gurdaspur in East Panjab, has a glorious history. The abandoned and neglected gardens were once lush and green with a myriad of trees, wild, colourful flowers, and sweet summer fruits. The old derelict houses with crumbling walls and no doors were once filled with the joyous laughter of children born to warriors, mystics, and rulers. Today, these overgrown gardens and dilapidated houses are just remnants of a bygone era, as poets and writers tried to preserve their past glory in the hope of reviving their true worth.

The homes were lined with marble floors and rich ornaments as the residents wore lavish clothes and expensive jewellery. The crowded streets flowed with skilled traders and inquisitive travellers. Kings, *Nawabs*, and *Sikh Sardars* once roamed this city, alongside Sants,

Yogis, and *Sadhus*. Many beautiful women arrived in this city in a grandiose manner as they began new lives with their chosen partners. These were happy and joyous times, but they did not last.

Over time the same women, who arrived as beautiful young wives and raised loving children, were seen running barefoot, out of those large houses that once offered so much comfort and protection. Instead of *sindoor* and elegant scarves, they were seen running in dirt, with their hair out and tears rolling down from their eyes. The lavish clothes that once wrapped their bodies were torn, and their necks and wrists lacked the sparkle of expensive jewellery. Helpless onlookers lowered their gazes as the women, many carrying their young infants, screamed and ran from their tormentors, thorns cutting through their feet as they fled across the gardens.

Homes were looted, and countless women caught in the shameless hands of men, overcome with lust, who devoured their bodies, cut apart their children, and killed their husbands. The women were paraded through the streets before being piled upon horse carts and taken back to foreign lands where they were sold like livestock and forced to convert.

Their lives were turned upside-down, and with the passing of time, their houses left in peril. In Batala today, their stories may have been relegated to the passages of history, but those homes, *havelis,* and gardens, while abandoned and derelict, stand as storehouses of their glory days.

It was 1885 when a foreign traveller, eager to explore the Majha region of Panjab, was passing through Batala. It was a warm and clear day; he had been on the go since 6 a.m. that morning. As the sun began to set, he passed by a group of abandoned houses with untidy gardens. He said to himself, "There is nothing here. There are just empty old buildings and overgrown gardens everywhere. What a dump! There's nothing to see here; perhaps I should just be on my way and head back for the day."

As he spoke these words, another, more assured voice called out, "Careful, son, you are but a guest here. Choose your words carefully, for you know nothing about the greatness of this city."

Turning around, the traveller saw a man, perhaps older than his own grandfather, leaning over with both hands resting on a wooden stick that was helping him stand. Before he could reply, the old man continued, "Have some shame, for it was your ancestors who destroyed the beauty and glory of this city! Like the Shalamar Bagh of Lahore, this city was home to many royal gardens and stunning architecture. There were many beautiful flowers and calming fountains dotted around where you stand today. From morning until night, great men, women, and children walked and played within these grounds. Don't be so quick to judge with the limits of your eyes. Upon closer inspection, you will see that these gardens hold stories of a glorious but unwritten past."

Glancing over at the gardens and then turning to the dilapidated houses in the distance, the traveller said, "Forgive me, *Baba ji,* I do not know what this place is. Who owns this land?"

"Well," began the *Baba,* "at the moment, I own this land, but during my grandfather's time, this land belonged to the Kanaiya Misl."

"The Kanaiya Misl?" the traveller asked. He vaguely remembered hearing about the Misls, of which there had been a total of twelve, who made up the Sikh confederacy of the late $18^{th}$ century.

"Yes. The gardens were established by Rani Sada Kaur of the Kanaiya Misl in memory of her late husband, Sardar Gurbaksh Singh. In her youth, she spent much of her time here. You see that mango tree over there? She planted that with her own hands. Over the years, she would sit under its shade and meditate on Vaheguru. It was in these very gardens that she learnt *Shastar Vidhia,* the science of weaponry. Those two buildings on that side, where owls now sit and hoot at night, they were where Rani Sada Kaur kept her horses."

"*Shastar Vidhia*? Horses?"

"Yes, son. Rani Sada Kaur was one of the most skilled and established warriors of her time. She had taken *Amrit*, the sweet nectar of immortality, prepared with the double-edged sword, and joined the *Khalsa* collective of Guru Gobind Singh at a young age. She was a fearless warrior who led thousands of men into battle. Her horses? She had two, Vayu and Gaggar; they were tall, strong, sturdy, and under Rani Sada Kaur's command galloped all over Panjab, from the Khyber Pass across to Ladakh and Manali!"

The *Baba*'s face lit up; he dropped the wooden stick and straightened his back. The traveller, himself almost six-feet tall, was suddenly dwarfed under the *Baba*'s shadow. Raising his large, strong hands and pointing towards the buildings, the *Baba* continued, "My grandfather, Kamanda Singh, looked after those horses. Oh, son! What can I tell you about those glorious days! Just thinking about the great souls who sat in these gardens gives me goosebumps. Sher Singh, too, spent his younger days playing in the laps of his grandmother. His father, Maharaja Ranjit Singh, held many *darbars* here. But ... but people now say this place is cursed, and many say they have seen spirits and ghosts roaming the grounds at night. After sunset, no one walks past here, son. But I have no fear; I often spend my nights here, thinking about my father, my grandfather, and the countless blessed souls who saw these gardens in all their glory."

Looking back at the traveller, the *Baba* paused for a moment and then continued, "I want to share one story with you, then you can be on your way."

Crossing his arms, the traveller nodded.

"It was late August, a few hours after sunset. Large, sweet mangoes were ripe and ready to be picked, and I noticed the hawk that had been encircling the place all day. I was lying on a *manja* just beside the old stables of Vayu and Gaggar. The clouds rumbled in the night sky. As I looked out, a flash of white light suddenly engulfed the entire garden. It was as if the moon was entering the earth's atmosphere. I sat up and watched as the light split into three separate orbs of light and slowly morphed into the shape of individual figures. I panicked and thought, *people were right, this area is cursed, ghosts do wander the gardens. Have they come to take me?* I was not much older than you, son."

The traveller continued to listen attentively.

"In a complete state of shock, I was unable to move from the *manja*. My eyes saw how one light formed into what appeared to be a man, floating some twelve inches off the ground; he had broad shoulders and was adorned with weapons. The second was a young child with her hair tied up in a top-knot and a garland of flowers around her neck. The third figure was a woman; she was tall and had the most powerful aura. They wandered all around the gardens and eventually came and stopped at this mango tree. I wanted to get up and run but was unable to move my body. I then saw how those ripe mangoes fell from the tree into the hands of the woman. They did not speak. They saw me but did not move towards me. Then, slowly, they moved back into the centre of the gardens, and just like that, merged back into the main light and vanished. After they left, there was complete darkness again. Then, it began to rain in a way that I have never seen before in my life."

The traveller had stood listening to the entire story. He looked over the gardens again and found himself wanting to know more about its former owners. Turning back to the *Baba,* the traveller eagerly asked, "So those three figures that you saw, who were they, *Baba ji*?"

"I have always believed them to have been Rani Sada Kaur, Raja Gurbaksh Singh, and their daughter Mehtab Kaur, who despite having left this world many years ago, came back to enjoy the fruits of their making. This mango tree stands as a constant reminder of them and their story."

"*Baba ji,* you are blessed for having experienced such a miracle. But please tell me, who was Rani Sada Kaur? Who was Raja Gurbaksh Singh, and what happened to their family?"

With that, the *Baba* picked up his walking stick, led the traveller to one side, and sat him down on an old *manja*. The *Baba*'s eyes sparkled, and his face glowed. As he sat the traveller down, *Baba* put his stick to one side. He was about to tell the story he had narrated to hundreds of travellers throughout his long life. The *Baba* had always gained much peace and happiness from telling this story, for he too had the blood of martyrs pumping through his veins.

As the traveller settled down, the *Baba* spoke, "Rani Sada Kaur, or Sardarni Sada Kaur as she was also known, was one of the most beautiful, brave, and courageous women to have lived in Panjab. She endured great hardship but had the foresight and political astuteness to raise the Lion of Panjab, Maharaja Ranjit Singh, and establish *Khalsa* Raj across all of Panjab. She was the embodiment of truth and compassion; both fearless and daring, she always stood for *dharam* and spent her entire life fighting those who opposed the universal teachings of Sikhi, such as equality, liberty, and freedom for all. If you truly wish to hear her story, then listen carefully; I will tell you."

# 2.

Rami came running down the street. She fell not once or twice, but several times. Her nose and mouth were bleeding, but she did not stop, even as the *chuni* from her head fell to one side. She was not a young child anymore, but a seventeen-year-old girl soon to become a young woman. She wanted to scream out what she had just heard but somehow was unable to find the words to voice it. Overcome with emotions of anger, shock, and dismay, Rami kept running.

Upon seeing Rami running through the streets, the locals of the town became worried. Some stepped back away from the main path, while others began closing their windows and doors.

"The fact Rami is running in such a state means something terrible has happened. After all, she is running from the direction of the battlefield!" observed one of the onlookers.

A couple of carpenters, who had heard the commotion from up the street, ventured forward and shouted, "Rami! Who won?"

"What happened to your face?"

"Why are you in such a hurry?"

But Rami ignored the questions and kept on running. She had to reach the palace. She had to see the queen.

As Rami turned the corner and entered the palace grounds, she once again fell over and this time injured her forehead, which instantly opened a wound, causing blood to trickle down her face. Despite the pain this caused, Rami picked herself up and continued to run towards the palace doors, knowing her message would deliver an even greater pain.

As she entered the courtyard and saw the familiar faces of the royal attendants, she could no longer keep it in, and despite her best efforts to prevent a scene, she instinctively screamed, *"Raja ji Shaheed hogay! Raja ji Shaheed hogay!"* The king has been martyred! The king has been martyred!

The words reverberated around the palace walls, instantly catching the courtiers' attention, men, women, and children. They all stopped what they were doing and let out shrieks of shock and horror.

"The king has been martyred! How can that be?"

"Yes, the king has been martyred," shouted Rami as blood trickled even faster down her face, turning the upper neckline of her bright *phulkari kurta* into a deep, crimson red.

A great commotion took over the palace, with many people in utter shock. Others, overcome with sadness, began to wail out in agony. Having heard the shouting and crying outside, the queen opened her doors and came down the stairs. Upon seeing her enter the courtyard, the womenfolk began to cry even louder.

Rami, who was fighting back the tears, slowly approached the queen and uttered, *"Rani ji haner hogia! Raja ji Shaheed hogay, Raja ji Shaheed hogay;"* O' my dear queen, darkness has befallen us, the king has been martyred! The king has been martyred!

The queen to whom Rami was speaking was none other than Rani Sada Kaur. Twenty-two years old, Sada Kaur was a tall and beautiful young woman; her face was ever-radiant, and the beauty of her eyes appeared supernatural. She was dressed in a traditional *kurta* and *salvar*, with a long, heavy shawl draped around her head and over her chest, with her right arm tucked in. On her wrists were gold bangles set against the sparkling jewellery around her neck and fingers.

As Sada Kaur stood there and listened to the words of her trusted aide, the realisation that the king, her husband, Sardar Gurbaksh Singh, had died in the battle for which he had left their palace that morning, slowly began to sink in. Turning towards the attendants and then back towards Rami, Sada Kaur asked, "Rami? What are you saying?"

"Rani ji, I am telling you the truth, the king has been martyred. The enemy has won. The king has fallen on the battlefield." Rami tried to explain the whole account.

"If the king has been martyred, then why have you caused such a scene? Why is everyone crying?"

Turning to the attendants in the courtyard, Sada Kaur said, "Tell me! Why are you crying?"

"He was our beloved king!" came a reply.

"He was so young, and now he has left us for good," came another voice.

"Stop this crying at once!" roared Sada Kaur.

"Those who march to war are destined for martyrdom. Those who become martyrs, they do not die - they become immortal. One should cry for those who sit at home and die from bad health or an illness. Those who wage war and die for the sake of righteousness and in protection of the weak, they alone can be said to have lived a true life. Please do not disturb my soul with your crying; stop this at once."

Everyone in the courtyard was silenced. Gradually, some of the womenfolk used their *chunia* to wipe away their tears. Slowly but surely, in the presence of Sada Kaur, the mood within the courtyard changed. There was a large portrait of the king, which caught one of the servant's attention, through the entrance doors behind Sada Kaur.

"He was so young, yet look at how much he achieved in such a short time. He was a strong and noble leader," she said.

At around six foot three, Gurbaksh Singh had broad shoulders, with a short beard and budding moustache. It had only been three years since his marriage to Sada Kaur, and they were both young and deeply in love. Where Gurbaksh Singh loved his wife, he also had a love for fighting with dignity and bravery on the battlefield, something Sada Kaur had always admired in her husband.

Rami accompanied Sada Kaur as she headed back towards her quarters. They walked in silence across the hallway and up the stairs. As they entered the room, Rami observed Sada Kaur pause and look over at the rich collection of Gurbaksh Singh's weapons, which hung all around the walls. Sada Kaur smiled and then, with her head held high, gracefully walked towards a heavy-looking sword. Placing the hilt in her hand, with one swooping move she unsheathed the sword, which emanated an electric radiance into the room.

Lowering her forehead to the blade in reverence, Sada Kaur closed her eyes and declared, "My dear husband, if it is true that you have attained martyrdom in battle, then I kiss this blade and vow with sword in hand that I will avenge your death. I will retake our lost territory from the hands of those who have become our enemies. I know in my heart you will support me from the presence of *Akal Purakh,* whom you are now with. *Kalgidhar Pita,* Sri Guru Gobind Singh, will give me the strength to deliver justice."

"Taking the support and shelter of only *Akal Purakh,* I shall bring glory to your name, as your beloved wife and heiress to the Kanaiya Misl."

With that, Sada Kaur respectfully lowered the sword. She walked over to the mirror, removed the shawl from around her neck, and tore it in half. Taking one half, she tied a *dumalla* on her head and then picked up the other half and tied it around her waist to form a *kamarkasa.* Taking the sword again, she turned to Rami and said, "You come with me. Basanti, Taro, Dharmo, and Kaliani will see to matters here. Please ask Kamanda Singh to fetch our horses as we are riding to the battlefield today - I wish to bring home the body of my beloved husband."

Upon saying this, Sada Kaur walked out of the room, with Rami following behind. A fearless rage was permeating from her face. She quickly came down from the top floor of the palace and ushered Rami to head on straight to the stables. Within a few minutes, Rami and Kamanda Singh re-entered the main courtyard with both horses. They climbed atop and swiftly rode out of the palace grounds.

As the horses trotted through the narrow streets towards the main pathway, people turned around and stopped to watch. This was the second time they had seen horses leave in such a hurry that day.

"Rani ji, are you heading to the battle?"

"Is it true, the king has been martyred?"

These were the common questions shouted out by those who deemed it unsafe to travel and instead had remained in the town. Unfazed, Rami and Sada Kaur rounded the streets and galloped off at full speed towards the battlefield of Achal.

# 3.

Achal is situated approximately three miles north of Batala, where an old *mandir* of *Shiv ji* is situated in the middle of a small reservoir of water. To the south of the reservoir is a *Gurdwara,* built in reverence of Guru Nanak Dev ji. Opposite the reservoir is an open field. This was the place that had just witnessed Raja Gurbaksh Singh's fall on the battlefield.

The sun was setting off to the west, and there were darker skies on the horizon to the east. Following Gurbaksh Singh's death, the commanders on both sides had pulled back their forces. As Sada Kaur and Rami rode onto the battlefield, they saw a blanket of bloodied bodies, many missing arms and legs, with many more laying headless. In the distance, Rami noticed how soldiers from either side were attending to their fallen brethren, trying to bandage the wounds of those who were still conscious and moving. Sada Kaur rode a little further before stopping and dismounting from her horse.

She stepped through the carpet of bodies that lay lifeless on the ground in search of her husband. She recognised some of the soldiers from the Kanaiya Misl. Where there lay one member of her Misl, there were a further three or four corpses of the enemy laying around him. She thought, *they all fought so valiantly, taking out many enemy soldiers before they fell.* Sada Kaur carefully and humbly manoeuvred through the pile of bodies until she recognised the body of Gurbaksh Singh.

With respect, Sada Kaur moved forward, lifted her husband up, and checked him from head to toe. In addition to four bullet wounds across his chest and left thigh, there were countless blade wounds all over his body. His clothes were drenched in blood, and his *dastaar* was dislodged, with his beautiful black mane draped over his shoulders. *My beloved fought heroically in his final stand,* thought Sada Kaur, before noticing Gurbaksh Singh's trustworthy horse too lay lifeless beside them.

Sada Kaur also saw the motionless bodies of at least eight enemy soldiers around her, most of whom had limbs missing. Their weapons were scattered around them, some still within the clenched fists of their dismembered hands. Looking back at Gurbaksh Singh's body, tears began to roll down Sada Kaur's face, falling onto the chest of her husband. Upon seeing her tears trickle down and drop onto the blood-soaked chest of her husband, Sada Kaur smiled and reassured herself; *you must stay strong. This is a moment of glory; just look at the battle wounds across Sardar ji's body.*

Sensing Rami walk towards her, Sada Kaur said, "These are tears of love and joy. They are an expression of my love, a deep yearning from my soul to meet with my beloved again soon."

"Rani ji watch out!" shouted Rami.

Sada Kaur looked up at Rami and then turned towards where she was pointing. She saw one of the enemy soldiers hobbling towards her, his sword raised over his head. Sada Kaur lowered her husband's head to the ground, then, in one sweeping move, swivelled on her resting foot to rise and unsheathe her sword. As she did so, the soldier's sword came crashing down and struck hers, but the blow made him lose his grip, and it fell out of his hand. Sada Kaur swung her sword in circular motion high into the air before bringing it back and taking the soldier's head clean off. As the head rolled off to the left, the body dropped down to its knees and collapsed in a heap at Sada Kaur's feet.

Rami and Sada Kaur scanned the battlefield around them for any others still alive, but no one else was moving. They vigilantly returned to the spot where Gurbaksh Singh lay. Sada Kaur picked up her husband's sword and shield.

She also recognised his rifle and the short dagger still clenched in his right hand.

Holding them tight, she proudly proclaimed, "O my dear husband, standing in this battlefield, I vow to shoulder the responsibility of raising the Misl up from this defeat. Those who have attacked us, without good reason but to simply take our rule, I will seek them out. I will retake what is rightfully ours and work to build a more prosperous Panjab. I will now adorn your weapons; they will protect my life and dignity. I vow to fight for the righteous cause and pledge to raise the sovereign flags of the *Khalsa* all over Panjab."

As Sada Kaur spoke these words, her father-in-law, Sardar Jai Singh, had slowly managed to find his way to her through the pile of bodies. His large frame was riddled with marks of battle, and he was also nursing an injury to his left shoulder. As was customary in those days, up until that point, Sada Kaur had only presented herself before her father-in-law in a veil. Jai Singh was taken aback when he saw Sada Kaur draped in weapons, her face glowing amidst the setting sun, and her sword drenched in blood.

"Sada Kaur, when did you arrive?" he asked.

"I came as soon as I heard the news, Father," said Sada Kaur, turning her head down towards Gurbaksh Singh.

"But your sword?" Jai Singh asked, pointing as the blood continued to drip down the blade.

"Yes, Father. It's all sorted; one of the enemy soldiers tried to attack us, but I took his head."

Appearing a little disorientated, Jai Singh then looked down at his son and, overcome with grief, threw himself on top of his lifeless body. He cried out, "My beloved son, this can't be! No, please wake up, my son! You cannot leave me now. I am very old; I need you! Who will take over as leader of the Misl? Is this now the end of the Kanaiya Misl? Will it fall into the hands of the enemy? Oh, dear son, please wake up, please tell me."

"Dear Father," spoke Sada Kaur, "there is no need to worry. From this day forward, I will take over from your son. Bearing the banners of the Kanaiya Misl, I will establish a stronger and greater rule for all of Panjab. If anyone dares to look towards us, I will remove their eyes! We must accept the Will of Vaheguru. The regretful matter in all of this is that, where we were supposed to fight off the advances of the Mughals and foreign adversaries, we will have to fight with our own lost brothers. A Singh should never have raised his hand towards another Singh, but we will need to finish this bitter quarrel once and for all."

Sada Kaur was referring to the actions of individual Misl Sardars, or chiefs, such as Jassa Singh Ramgharia and Maha Singh, who had colluded with Sansar Chand to take down the growing influence of the Kanaiya Misl in the Majha region of Panjab. They had allowed their own egos to get the better of them and created divisions amongst the Sikhs. While the Misls had previously emerged as a natural progression of the Guru's mandate to pursue and establish political autonomy, they also existed to withstand the oppression of Mughal and foreign attacks in which the Sikhs had endured two huge holocausts. The overall objective of the Misls was the same, and their claims to sovereignty were bestowed by the same source; upon capturing power, however, some had lost their way and had begun chasing power for personal and familial aims, at the expense of the Sikh nation's wider political objectives.

Jai Singh looked up at Sada Kaur. There was defiance in her eyes that he had never seen before. She stood tall, like a warrior goddess of old legends. For the first time, he sensed a strong, brave soul was sitting within the body of his daughter-in-law. He thought for a moment and then, holding his injured shoulder, he spoke, "Okay, dear. Whatever *Akal Purakh* wishes is acceptable to me. May he bless us all with the strength and the conviction to establish *Khalsa Raj*. All the soldiers of the Kanaiya Misl will work to support you."

Accepting the blessings, Sada Kaur bowed her head in reverence and then walked over to her horse. She tied up some of her husband's weapons and then called over a few of the remaining Kanaiya soldiers. Together, they piled up the bodies of the martyred Singhs before Sada Kaur performed the *Antim Ardas,* the final prayer in which she recalled the Guru's Words:

*Death is pre-ordained – no one who comes can remain here.*

Sada Kaur also meditated on the Guru's teachings that say the soul itself is not subject to the cycle of birth and death. Death is only the progression of the soul on its journey into the next world. If the soul has achieved what it arrived on earth to obtain, then it merges back into the supreme soul. In life, a Sikh is instructed always to remember death so that he or she may be adequately detached and ready to break the cycle of birth and death and merge back into Vaheguru.

Gurbaksh Singh's body was raised into a palanquin and then lifted by some of the soldiers. Sada Kaur, Rami, Jai Singh, and the remaining soldiers mounted their horses and rode beside the palanquin. The sun had disappeared into the night sky. They all walked through the dark in silence; only the hooves of the horses striking the ground could be heard.

# 4.

In the district of Lahore lies the town of Kahna. This is where Sardar Kushal Singh lived, with his sons Sangha Singh, Jhanda Singh, and Jai Singh, the youngest. Jai Singh was a tall, well-built, and handsome young man. In his youth, he was nicknamed 'Krishan-Kanaiya,' which is why when the Misls arose, he became known as the Kanaiya Misl leader.

Jai Singh was bestowed with *Amrit* by the famous Nawab Kapur Singh, founder of the *Dal Khalsa,* a fierce fighting force with two main branches - the *Taruna Dal* and the *Budha Dal.* From within the *Taruna* Dal, the first five Misls evolved, soon becoming twelve towards the end of the 18$^{th}$ century. Each Misl laid claim to certain territory and formed an integral part of the wider Sikh confederacy.

In his youth Jai Singh spent much time within the *Dal Khalsa,* displaying feats of bravery. He rode into Sohia, the town of his in-laws, with four-hundred horsemen. Sohia lay in the district of *Amrit*sar, and Jai Singh quickly won over the locals and established his rule. Over a short time, he won over Batala, Pathankot, Makeria, and the areas between the Rivers Ravi and Beas.

In February 1785, Jassa Singh Ramgharia, along with Sansar Chand Katochia and Maha Singh Sukerchakia, had combined their forces and fought with Jai Singh in Batala. This was the battle in which Jai Singh's son, Gurbaksh Singh, had attained martyrdom. Jassa Singh and Sansar Chand had taken over Pathankot, leaving Jai Singh with Batala and Sohia. The loss of his youngest son had a big impact on Jai Singh.

Whilst Jai Singh had two other sons, he had developed a special bond with Gurbaksh Singh, but his death, alongside the realisation that his Misl had just lost large territory, was further cause for concern. He was getting quite old now, too, and the thought of having no obvious candidate to take over the reins was eating away at Jai Singh.

One day, shortly after the battle, Jai Singh was sat alone in his library. His mind was racing, and he was both anxious and fearful of what lay ahead. He stood up and began to pace around the room, trying to process the thoughts running through his mind. His eyes shot around the room, scanning his weapons, which hung on the wall, the large stack of books piled upon his desk, the various ornaments scattered around the room. Then he stared out of the open window, looking into the distant fields. He no longer found solace in the items that had once brought him so much joy and fulfilment. His sword, which had once lit up battlefields across the region, hung high above the mantlepiece, but it now appeared dreary, like it had lost its shine. The books he had read as a budding astrologer no longer seemed to contain the words that once inspired him.

*Time has betrayed me*, he thought.

"If my son were alive, I would never have seen this day. This day of defeat. How will I regain the expanse of my lost rule?" he said aloud to himself.

"The rule will return. Raj comes to those who have the strength of will and determination," said a voice.

Jai Singh turned around and saw a figure standing in the doorway of the library. He stepped back and rubbed his eyes. For a moment, he thought it was his son; moving back, he stumbled and said, "My child, is that you? What are you doing here?"

"Yes, Father, it is I, Sada Kaur," came the reply.

Sada Kaur was dressed from head to toe in full battle gear, adorned with her late husband's weapons. She had tied a *dumalla* upon her head and had a *kamarkasa* around her waist in which she had placed some smaller hand weapons.

"I have gathered three hundred horsemen. We shall ride over our towns and fight off the thieves who are harassing our people," said Sada Kaur powerfully.

"*Kalgidhar Pita,* Guru Gobind Singh, rider of the blue horse, will provide the way. As his daughter, I know in my heart I have the support I need. We will create a new Panjab and establish a great Raj," she continued with conviction.

As her eyes pierced across the room, with sword in hand, she was a sight to behold.

"May *Akal Purakh* be with you, but ..." started Jai Singh, unable to finish his sentence.

"But what, Father? Why did you stop? Please complete your words," said Sada Kaur.

"My dear child, you are the daughter of a brave warrior, the wife of a valiant martyr, and the daughter-in-law of Jai Singh. Within your blood is the strength and conviction of many great warriors, but you are just a woman," he replied.

"I am not just a woman. I am a *Singhni.* With the Grace of Vaheguru, I consider the Guru to be *'Ang Sang,'* forever with me. Victory is guaranteed by the sword of Guru Nanak. I will rule in good faith and consider the welfare of all. Beyond Guru and the Creator, I fear no man or woman alive. As founder of this great Misl, I just need your blessings," roared back Sada Kaur.

"Dear, please sit down ..." began Jai Singh.

"... you must understand the seriousness of the matter at hand. This is governance and warfare of the highest order. Before you came here today, my mind was riddled with anxiety. I was thinking about Gurbaksh Singh and how strong and able a leader he was. If only he were still alive, you could have ridden out together. Those who stand in our way today should never have become our enemies. We have faltered in our pledge to Guru Gobind Singh. We have been enticed by the lure of worldly status and lost our way."

Jai Singh continued, "I have only come to realise this after the martyrdom of Gurbaksh Singh. Our objective was to spread Sikhi, challenge tyranny, and uphold Sikh sovereignty. We should never have fought with one another. I am now old, and as an old man with no heir in sight, I do not know what will come of our Misl."

As Jai Singh narrated the sorrows of his mind's condition, Sada Kaur's blood was boiling. Her body was full of rage, and in one swift move, she unsheathed her sword, which lit up the room like a bolt of lightning.

Placing her forehead on the sword, Sada Kaur, in a state of fearless love, loudly proclaimed, "Dear Father, I vow on the sword of my husband to establish the Khalsa Raj, which Guru Gobind Singh ordained the *Khalsa* to build when they sent Banda Singh Bahadur to march on Sirhind. No one will go hungry; no one will be without shelter and clothing. I will build a powerful Raj, raising the sovereign flags of the *Guru Khalsa* across the land of the five rivers. I shall march upon the enemy, with *Gurbani* on my lips, and war on my mind."

Jai Singh fell silent. Unable to offer any response, he watched and listened as Sada Kaur continued, "I was born a woman, but I have tasted *Amrit* from the iron bowl, prepared with the double-edged sword. From that moment forward, I became a beloved daughter of Guru Gobind Singh and pledged to advance the Khalsa Panth. Listen, O' Father, mountains may eventually fall, the earth may drop from its rotational axis, the moon and sun may never rise again, but the Guru's Word will always remain. As a *Singhni* of *Kalgidhar Patshah,* I cannot go against the pledge I made in front of the *Panj Pyar-e,* the Beloved Five," continued Sada Kaur.

"With respect and humility, I ask again for your blessings. Do not think I am 'just a woman,' or the daughter of the brave Dasvandha Singh, widow of Gurbaksh Singh and daughter-in-law of Jai Singh. No! I ask you to see me as the *Singhni* of Guru Gobind Singh that I proudly am. I take inspiration from other fearless *Singhnia* who have walked before me, like Bibi Bhago, who not only re-awoke the forty that had left Guru Sahib but led them back into battle; or Bibi Sharan Kaur, who honourably stood and performed the final rites of the martyrs in the Battle of Chamkaur, despite the imminent threat to her own life. As a Sikh of the Guru, I am not afraid of death. I will send death to the doors of our enemies!"

Overcome with a new sense of pride and belief, Jai Singh awoke from his sorrowful state. Sada Kaur's presence and words had given him new hope. She reminded him of his younger self. Raising his hand, Jai Singh blessed Sada Kaur to proceed forward.

Sada Kaur placed her sword back into the sheath and, with respect, took up *Bir Asan*, the warrior's pose, and bowed in front of Jai Singh.

Touching his feet, she declared, "Dear Father, my head bows towards you, as founder of this Misl - it shall never bow before any other man or government."

Pleased with Sada Kaur's wisdom and desire to capture political power for the Khalsa, Jai Singh smiled.

"Well done, dear. Now I feel like I can walk with my head held high. Knowing your heart is in the right place, with the Grace of Vaheguru, you shall be guided to victory. Go now, march on the enemies of the Panth and unite the glorious land of our Gurus. All glory be to Guru and *Akal Purakh.*"

Jai Singh called for Dal Singh, the commander-in-chief of his army, and told him, "From this moment forward, Sada Kaur is the leader - you must support her in every course of action."

Turning again to Sada Kaur he said, "These eyes may not live to see the day you unite all of Panjab, but my spirit will forever yearn to see the reign of the Khalsa. Go now my child, Akal Sahai."

# 5.

Sada Kaur was born in 1762. Her father's name was Dasvandha Singh, a brave warrior who served in the *Dal Khalsa*. Both Jai Singh and Dasvandha Singh were friends, and they turned their friendship into an alliance with the marriage of Gurbaksh Singh and Sada Kaur.

From a young age, alongside learning Gurmukhi, Sada Kaur always took a keen interest in her father's military expertise. She was raised well by her parents, who were both loving and responsible for their daughter. A child's first school is held by the parents, and the lessons they teach go with the child into adulthood. In the loving presence of her parents, Sada Kaur learned about the glorious actions of the Guru and the Guru's Beloved. She was inspired by her ancestors' bravery and courage, the stories of whom she grew up hearing.

There is much responsibility on the parents to raise their child well; if they neglect or pass on bad habits to their child, this leaves a lasting impression on how the child develops. However, Sada Kaur was blessed with parents who taught her well.

By the time Sada Kaur turned twelve, she had memorised many *Shabads* from Guru Granth Sahib. Her daily *rehat,* discipline, included rising early, reciting *Gurbani,* meditating, and then studying until the afternoon. She was not like the other children in her village. While they studied too, Sada Kaur would spend an extra few hours with her books before joining them to play.

In addition to *Dharmic* Studies, she began her physical training in *Shastar Vidhia* and soon mastered the sword and horse riding. In those days, the children of Sikhs were taught to master both the pen and the sword from a very young age, and by the time Sada Kaur had turned sixteen, she was a well-trained rider and carrier of the sword. The Sikhs considered such training to be their basic life skills, as per the Guru's instructions. Because of their training and love for *Shastar Vidhia,* they were able to endure the onslaught of two genocides that century.

Often, Sada Kaur would ride many kilometres out of her village and spend time in the forest, riding her horse through the wilderness. Her love for Sikhi had created a strong bond with *Gurbani.* She would sing and contemplate the Guru's Word as she spent time in nature. Due to her upbringing, Sada Kaur was very strong in both mind and body.

On one occasion in the winter of 1778, Sada Kaur was travelling home to Dhariwal, which lay some twenty-five kilometres south west of Batala. As she rode through Qadian back to Dhariwal, Sada Kaur saw a unit of Singhs on horseback marching from the direction of Batala.

"Sarkar Jai Singh has reigned victorious in the battle," proclaimed one of the riders.

Sada Kaur inquisitively asked, "Brother, which battle are you referring to?"

The Singh informed Sada Kaur of the hotly contested battles that had taken place in Hargobindpura, Kalanaur and Batala, between the coalition of Sardars Jai Singh, Haqiqat Singh, and Gurbaksh Singh of the Kaniaya Misl, Jassa Singh Ahluwalia, Maha Singh Sukerchakia, and Sansar Chand against the Ramgharia Misl, headed by Jassa Singh Ramgharia. The defeat for the Ramgharias had forced them to leave and head south to the territory of Hisar, near Delhi.

Sada Kaur listened to the Singh as he explained how the battles unfolded and what this victory meant for the Kaniaya and Sukerchakia Misls, who were both jostling for power in Panjab. While Sada Kaur had heard her father speak about Jai Singh and Maha Singh, she was also familiar with the names of the two Jassa Singhs, who were regarded as some of the most skilled warriors in all of Panjab.

Although Sada Kaur was only sixteen years old, she had already developed a deep love and affiliation to the Khalsa Panth. The news of these battles saddened her, especially because Jassa Singh Ramgharia was the grandson of *Baba* Hardas Singh, one of Guru Gobind Singh's main court writers.

*How far have we fallen in just seventy years?* she thought. *The Guru bestowed us with sovereignty, but in our efforts to ward off foreign invaders and stand against injustice, we have fallen prey to the lures of temporal governance. This is not sustainable. When infighting becomes too rife between brothers, the family is eventually uprooted. There needs to be a change. As the Khalsa, we must do better.*

Sada Kaur's growth and development into a strong and beautiful young woman did not go unnoticed. Many people in the village admired her for both her skills and her natural beauty. Sardar Jai Singh had been informed of Sada Kaur's unique qualities and her fearless courage. Within the few months following her sixteenth birthday, he approached Sardar Dasvandha Singh and asked for Sada Kaur to be married to his son, Gurbaksh Singh. Dasvandha Singh, too was fond of Gurbaksh Singh and very happy with the prospect of forming an alliance with the Kaniaya Misl, so he agreed.

Gurbaksh Singh was born in 1759 and was around nineteen years old when he married Sada Kaur. He, too, was a brave and courageous soul, and in many ways, the pair were made for each other. Sada Kaur and Gurbaksh Singh had one daughter, Mehtab Kaur, who truly lived up to her name (light of a candle). They were a caring young family who loved each other very much. If Gurbaksh Singh had not attained martyrdom in Achal, he would surely have gone on to become one of the most famous Sikhs of the 18th century, but such was the Will of Vaheguru that he passed on at the young age of twenty-four.

Following his passing, the thought of committing *sati* did not enter Sada Kaur's mind at all. *Sati* was a common cultural practice in those days where the widow would jump into the burning pyre at her husband's funeral. However, Sada Kaur was a *Singhni* well versed in *Gurbani,* which speaks out against such acts. As such, she was empowered to continue supporting her daughter and the Kanaiya Misl, which now rested upon her shoulders. She vowed at her husband's funeral to pick up his sword, adorn his armour, and continue the fight so that one day she could help create *Khalsa Raj* all over Panjab. Aware of the political reality, she had complete faith in *Kalgidhar Pita,* who would support her endeavours to create a better society for everyone.

Sada Kaur had completed an *Ardas* in which she had evoked the blessings of *Akal Purakh* Vaheguru and had undertaken an oath to uphold the sacred and sovereign duty of a daughter of Guru Gobind Singh. An *Ardas* completed with a pure thought is always answered - the power of *Akal Purakh* awakens and delivers on the *Ardas*.

Jai Singh had already given his blessings and assigned his top commanders to obey Sada Kaur's orders. As Sada Kaur marched with a contingent of approximately 300 horsemen, on her left flank was the mighty Dal Singh, who carried the Nishaan Sahib, and on Sada Kaur's immediate right, Rami, her trusted aide, rode alongside her.

As they galloped through different villages and towns, Sada Kaur thought about the daring adventures of Banda Singh Bahadur, who in 1708 had left Nander in the south and rode north to the plains of Panjab. He had been ordained and blessed by Guru Gobind Singh himself to march on Sirhind and avenge the murder of the Guru's four sons. Together with five sacred weapons and a small contingent of prominent warriors, Banda Singh left Nander and began delivering justice. He led the Khalsa warriors and annihilated those who had attacked Anandpur Sahib and deceived the Sikhs, in which times countless had perished. Within two years, Banda Singh raised the Khalsa flags and began minting coins in the Guru's name. Hundreds and thousands flocked to join him as he expanded the Khalsa Republic.

Sada Kaur was particularly inspired by the events that led to the rise of Banda, going back to the Battle of

Chamkaur. Her mother had narrated the story to her many times when she was younger, and each time Sada Kaur would hope that one day she could follow in the footsteps of her great ancestors. The triumphs of the battle in which approximately forty Singhs had withstood the might of an entire empire, much larger and more resourceful than them, were firmly entrenched in her mind. She was particularly moved by the fact they had been under siege for months, away from their families and the familiar surroundings of Anandpur. Despite this, each one had fought with honour and upheld the high battle standards of the Khalsa.

Sada Kaur envisioned that whole period - from when Guru Sahib was forced to leave Anandpur Sahib; the separation from his mother and two younger sons, and the thought of all the literature and treasures from the Guru's *Darbar* that were lost in the Sirsa River was a constant reminder of how much the Guru endured. She, too, had felt the pain of separation and loss. While trying to process the loss of her husband, Sada Kaur found comfort in the actions of her great ancestors. She took pride in knowing that her husband, too, had fought valiantly and joined them in the long line of Sikh martyrs.

Whenever her contingent stopped to rest, all manner of help was provided by them to the locals. Sometimes this help came in the form of money to farmers whose crops had been damaged; sometimes, clothes were provided for those who were unable to provide for themselves, and other times, Sada Kaur's contingent defended the locals against the advances of thieves and robbers.

Dal Singh was a formidable fighter; he would carve through the enemy with ease. They had trained together like siblings when they were younger, and both of them continuously encouraged one another to become better fighters. Much like Sada Kaur, Dal Singh could slice a man in half with one single strike of his sword. While he was an inspiration for the Singhs in his unit and led by example with the *tegh,* his sword, he was also at the forefront of leading the service of *degh,* food made in the Guru's communal kitchen.

Wherever they marched, once the miscreants and thieves had been removed, then Sada Kaur and Dal Singh set up large communal kitchens, serving *degh* to all. Upon seeing this dispensation of justice, many people began singing Sada Kaur's praises. The setting up of *degh* and *Langar* provided a much-needed service for the poor and needy. Everyone was treated equally and provided further items to help set up their own streams of income. The villages and towns that Sada Kaur liberated began to prosper, and news soon began to filter out into other districts.

# 6.

In September 1787, Jai Singh held a large *mela* for local youth. A special invitation was sent to those with a keen interest in sports, wrestling, and training. In the *mela,* Jai Singh set up various competitions - horse riding, *sochi, kabaddi,* sprinting, climbing, and sword duels. This *mela* was held over two days, with the winner in each competition receiving a prize.

One of the main reasons why Jai Singh held this large *mela* was to recruit strong and able fighters into his army. The *mela* was a huge success, and Jai Singh was able to add a thousand more soldiers to bolster the fighter force of the Kanaiya Misl.

A day after the *mela,* Jai Singh asked Sada Kaur to join him in the gardens of the *haveli* in Batala. He wanted to share some news with her.

"My daughter, I have made a decision," he started.

"What decision is that, dear Father?" enquired Sada Kaur.

"I have decided to form an alliance with Maha Singh, the head of the Sukerchakia Misl."

"Why, Father?"

"Well, to start with, this Misl is very powerful. They have great strength within their fighting force. They are also our enemy. Despite your efforts, and please understand I am fully with you, I am still fearful they may conquer our dominion following my death and imprison you," explained Jai Singh.

"Dear Father, Vaheguru is with me; I am not afraid of the likes of Maha Singh, Sansar Chand, or indeed any of the other Sardars. To speak of them capturing me or stopping me is one thing, but I assure you, I will not allow that to happen. Please do not weaken yourself with this speech; stay in *Chardikala,*" replied Sada Kaur.

"Well done, my child! I commend you for your spirit, but please listen to my whole idea. In politics, you must listen attentively to the other. Before replying, allow them to finish what they have to say," stated Jai Singh.

"Yes, Father, please continue."

"Maha Singh has a son, Ranjit Singh."

"Yes, that is right," Sada Kaur said with a nod.

"I wish to form an alliance between our Misls based on marrying your daughter, Mehtab Kaur, with Ranjit Singh. If the Kaniaya and Sukerchakia Misls forged together, we would become the most powerful force in all of Panjab. None of the other Misls would dare to attack us," explained Jai Singh.

He went on, "You may be a strong and courageous leader, Sada Kaur, but you need a big army to establish *Khalsa Raj*. Political rule is not possible without a strong and able army, my dear."

"Dear Father, you know how much I respect you and listen to your advice. But this is the same Maha Singh who colluded with our enemies and killed my husband on the battlefield. He is responsible for taking your son's life and capturing our land; if I ask for his son to marry my daughter, is this not a sign of weakness? The only common understanding we share is with the striking of our swords on the battlefield. Weak Rajputs would offer their daughters for marriage to the Mughals; were they right for doing this?" Sada Kaur questioned why Jai Singh had suggested the idea.

"Sada Kaur, there is a big difference between the Rajput and Mughal alliance and the relationship we have with the other Sikh Sardars. The comparison simply cannot be made," said Jai Singh.

Sada Kaur questioned why there was a difference between what Jai Singh was suggesting, and what the Rajputs had done with the Mughals.

"Listen dear! The Mughals were foreign invaders, whereas the Rajputs were of this land. They did not unite in their stand against the invaders but individually jostled for power. To save their own lives and cement their own position, they betrayed the siblings of their own motherland, which worked to the foreign invaders' advantage. But this is not what I am suggesting. On the contrary, this is about uniting our Sikh brothers and sisters, who have been led astray. We have to remember that Maha Singh is also a Sikh of the Guru - he too has drunk *Amrit* and pledged allegiance to the Khalsa. As a son of Panjab, he is like our own - he is not a foreign invader with ulterior motives. We should always strive to seek the best for our siblings, for we are like one big family; if one member is upset with you or even angry, we should try to resolve the issue, especially since it could further the political ambitions of the Khalsa Panth."

Looking down at his hands, Jai Singh spoke calmy and softly now.

"It is true, that once upon a time, Maha Singh was a very close friend of mine. We were both blessed with *Amrit* from the hands of Jathedar Nawab Kapur Singh. It is just unfortunate that he became greedy in the pursuit of Raj."

It was true; the Misls were formed out of political necessity and survival. The foreign invasions from Afghani kings and rulers had plunged Panjab into chaos and anarchy. The Marathas and Mughals too posed a threat to peace and stability in Panjab. Out of the quadruple struggle for political power, the Sikhs were considered the weakest party, but through sheer determined resistance, unity of Panthic purpose, and tenacity of will, they were victorious.

Once in charge of large territories, the Misls slowly but surely evolved into a system that was governed by the central assembly of a *Gurmata.* However, the pursuit of personal political ambition had caused a rift in the unity of the Misls. A new system was needed.

Upon hearing this, Sada Kaur thought for a moment and then replied, "I understand how we can change all of that. As you said, this alliance has the potential to unite all of the Panjab and mark the beginnings of the most glorious Raj that Panjab has seen. In Satguru's Name, we shall mint coins, strike the *Ranjit Nagara,* and raise the Sovereign Flags of the Guru Khalsa Panth."

"Exactly!" exclaimed Jai Singh. "The Misls have served their purpose, and if we do not evolve and adapt our ways, there will be no end to the infighting."

The other matter that was troubling Sada Kaur was the exploitative manner in which a new set of foreign invaders were strangling the regions around them. The British, who had been in South Asia since the 1600s, had recently become more aggressive in their extraction of resources and pursuit of territory. Bengal had fallen to the British following the Battle of Plassey (1757), and the British had also nullified French political ambitions in South Asia through a series of battles, which allowed them to coerce small regional rulers. A major battle (1782) had already been fought with the Maratha Empire, and while the Treaty of Salbai had calmed matters, further wars were anticipated by both sides.

They were a growing threat, and Sada Kaur was fully aware of this. Panjab was entering the dawn of a new political world, and she was determined to create a unified stand to prevent the British from entering the land of the five rivers.

With that in mind, both Sada Kaur and Jai Singh agreed to act promptly. Jai Singh summoned Dal Singh to go as an envoy and present the offer to Maha Singh, which he duly acted upon. Dal Singh returned after eight days with the news:

"Sardar Maha Singh and his wife, Raj Kaur, have agreed to the marriage of their son, Ranjit Singh, and our Mehtab Kaur."

Jai Singh was very pleased upon hearing this news. He turned to Sada Kaur and told her that although the children were still very young, it was comforting to know they had a bright future. They planned to marry the two when they were older.

Despite Jai Singh's elaborate plan, which filled him with much joy, he did not go on to see the wedding as he died a few years after this arrangement was made. His death had a deep impact upon Sada Kaur. Since her husband's death and her rise to the chief of the Misl, Jai Singh had offered wise counsel in times of difficulty. She missed him dearly but knew deep inside that she had to remain strong. The foreign invaders from the far west were waiting for an opportunity to pounce on the rich and fertile land of Panjab, but Sada Kaur had plans of her own.

# 7.

It was early spring of 1793. The stars shone bright in the night sky as *Amrit Vela* arrived. There were peace and tranquillity in the air. The *manmukhs,* egoists, were in a deep sleep; however, the *Gurmukhs* and the Sants were awake, in deep remembrance of their beloved Creator. Blessed are those souls who rise in the early hours to meditate on Vaheguru.

Sada Kaur, too was awake and sat cross-legged on the open veranda of her palace. Her eyes were closed with a *mala,* rosary beads in her left hand, and a *kirpan* that lay in its scabbard close by to her right hand. She was emerged in *Simran.* This was part of her daily *Sadhana,* spiritual discipline, something that Sada Kaur had developed during her childhood.

Although Sada Kaur had recited *Gurbani* from a young age, recently, she had developed a deeper, more profound connection during her daily *Sadhana.* She had full faith in the support of *Akal Purakh,* as she experienced much bliss during her *Simran.* Upon completely her *Nitnem,* morning prayers, and *Simran,* she stood up and began her *Ardas,* with a very particular thought in mind.

She stood with her hands tightly clasped in front of her, like those great warriors who had stood before major battles. With full attention and a pure mind, Sada Kaur freely recited *Gurbani,* seeking the blessings of *Akal Purakh.* She moved effortlessly, linking various *Shabads* from Guru Granth Sahib and Dasam Granth. Imbued with love and bliss, in one breath, she exclaimed, "Vaheguru."

At that precise moment, Sada Kaur entered a deeper consciousness. She felt a great energy close by; a power and frequency she had not experienced before. She felt weightless, almost like she was floating on thin air. She opened her eyes and saw a bright ball of light presenting itself before her. As the light took form right before her eyes, Sada Kaur saw a figure emerge. There was a royal *Kalgi,* plume, sitting majestically on the *dastaar.* She saw the beautiful beard, a flowing blue *chola* and an unsheathed *kirpan* that glistened in the night sky. Seeing all of this, Sada Kaur remained absorbed in a tranquil state and heard the following words:

"My daughter, pick up your sword, and all your tasks shall be completed. You have honest and noble intentions. You are the fire, the *Chandi;* you are a *Singhni;* victory will fall at your feet. The enemies will respect you. If you step on the lion's chest, you shall silence its roar. The country is calling out for you. Protect the weak and oppressed peoples of the land."

Sada Kaur then felt the light of pure energy surround her entire being. She closed her eyes and felt a sudden detachment, one which she had never experienced before. She no longer felt the ground beneath her feet, nor did she feel the weight of gravity pushing down from above. Opening her eyes, she saw her physical body standing on the ground, eyes closed, and surrounded by the light. As Sada Kaur turned around to try and gather her bearings, she looked down to find herself hovering above a battlefield. This was a battlefield she had not seen before, but one that she instantly recognised.

There was a fortress on the banks of the Yamuna River, where Singhs clad in iron and blue dress were preparing for a battle. Sada Kaur turned to her left, and in the distance, saw an army led by Fateh Shah, King of Sri Nagar, heading towards the fortress, which was named Paonta Sahib. They stopped and encamped some kilometres outside; a single horseman was then seen riding across to Poanta Sahib. He exchanged some words with a Singh who had ridden in from the right. Both men then turned around and headed into their own camps. Sada Kaur then watched as the Singh galloped back and bowed in front of the figure she had just seen during her *Ardas*. There was a beautiful white hawk perched on his shoulder. Sada Kaur understood where she was and what was happening. That was Guru Gobind Singh, and this was the commencement of the Battle of Bhangani, 1688.

The entire battle played out in front of her eyes, just as Kavi Sainapat had described in Sri Gur Sobha. After the Singh delivered his message, Guru Gobind Singh mounted his blue horse and marched to the battlefield with Nishaan Sahibs hoisted high above. Upon reaching the battlefield, Guru Sahib examined the enemy's positions and then deployed his Misls to take up their places around the enemy.

There were, in fact, eleven Misls under the command of Guru Gobind Singh, five of whom were headed up by the Guru's own cousins; Sango Shah, Jitmal, Sangat Rai, and Hari Chand - sons of Bibi Viro (the sister of Guru Tegh Bahudur). Gulab Rai, great-grandson of Guru Hargobind Sahib, was the head of a fifth Misl. Five further Misls were under the command of Pir Budhu Shah and his four sons, and the eleventh Misl was under the direct command of Guru Gobind Singh. The formation of the Misls was such that Guru Gobind Singh led from the centre, with his five cousins leading their units from the right wing, and Pir Budhu Shah and his sons leading the left wing. Sada Kaur watched the epic battle scene with a bird's eye view.

Sada Kaur also spotted, on the Guru's side, the Guru's maternal uncle Kirpal Das and Lal Chand, the son of Bidhi Chand, the beloved Gursikh of Guru Hargobind Sahib.

Fateh Shah of Sri Nagar was joined by other prominent Hindu Hill Chiefs such as Hari Chand Handooria and Bhim Chand of Bilaspur, as well as Mughal troops under Najabat Khan and Bhikham Khan.

*Nagaray* were played, the *narsingha* was blown, battle standards raised, and the Guru entered the battlefield. On the other side, Fateh Shah, having deployed his armed forces, stood firm and confident of victory. Beside him stood some of the most feared generals of the Hindu Hill Chiefs. In an instant, his forces began their charge towards the Guru and his Singhs. Both sides wielded their weapons and clashed most spectacularly. It was complete carnage; heads rolled from the first impact. The Guru's right flank was the most ferocious, pouncing on Fateh Shah's men like lions attacking their prey. Brandishing their swords, they pierced through many warriors. As a moth hovers around a lamp, unafraid of being struck down, such was the manner of the Singhs' movements. Sada Kaur saw a Singh slice a rival's body in two before cutting those pieces into four.

Another Singh on the right flank battled in the same manner, wielding his sword hard and fast. As he struck a blow on the approaching rider's head, he threw the sliced body to the ground. As he made mincemeat of the sliced bodies, he created such awe and terror on the battlefield that there was instant desertion from the enemy. That Singh of the Guru was acknowledged as the messenger of death on the battlefield.

In this manner, those ferocious Singhs, under the command of the Guru's cousins, continued to wreak havoc upon Fateh Shah's men. Sada Kaur saw another wide-eyed Singh launch a barrage of arrows, which plunged into an entire enemy battalion. Cries of desperation were heard from Fateh Shah's side, as many of his troops met the wrath of Guru Gobind Singh's warriors. Corpses upon corpses were piled up in heaps, and fountains of blood burst forth from the dead bodies.

Kirpal Das, the Guru's maternal uncle, routed out the famed Hayat Khan and killed him with a mighty blow. Other bodies were seen flying through the air before falling into a gorge on the side. Fateh Shah's men had never encountered such warriors; even as they outnumbered the Guru's forces, they were overwhelmed by the Singhs who encircled them like swarming locusts taking to a field of crops.

As the battle raged through its first phase, some of the Guru's faithful were struck with blows. With dagger in hand, Nand Chand carved through the enemy but was struck with a mighty blow. He fell to the ground, wounded, but was saved by the Guru. Despite the losses, the Guru's brave warriors battled on. Sango Shah was seen displaying such great feats of bravery that his actions were more daring than even the greatest warriors in Mahabharat. The arrogant and ego-fuelled soldiers who had arrived under Fateh Shah were routed by the prowling lions who charged through the battlefield.

Sada Kaur then saw Jitmal attain martyrdom at the hands of Hari Chand, the Hindu Hill Chief of Handoor. As she scanned the battlefield, Sango Shah, who had fought so valiantly, was martyred just after he killed Najabat Khan, the Pathan who had deserted Guru Gobind Singh's army before this battle. Sango Shah was later renamed Shah Sangram, the 'Monarch of War', by Guru Gobind Singh, for his acts of valour and bravery.

With two of the Guru's cousins and commanders of the right flanks falling, the Guru unleashed his wrath. Firing a barrage of arrows, he killed Bhikan Khan, another Pathan deserter. Sada Kaur then witnessed Hari Chand re-enter the battle. He strung an arrow upon his bow and fired towards the Guru. The arrow missed but was shortly followed by another, which scraped off the Guru's steel body armour. Guru Gobind Singh then loaded his bow and fired a barrage of arrows towards Hari Chand. The Hill Chief of Handoor was instantly killed alongside two of his generals.

Following this decisive blow, the remaining combatants of Fateh Shah's army deserted the field. Trumpets of victory sounded from the Guru's camp. Sada Kaur saw as a wave of joy spread amongst the Guru's faithful; they encircled the Guru and roared battle cries of victory:

"Bole So Nihal, Sat Sri Akal!!"

This was the Guru's first battle; as echoes of victory reverberated throughout the three worlds, Sada Kaur left her vantage point and returned to her body, which still stood in the *Ardas*. As the light vanished before her, she uttered, "*Dhan Kalgiawale Patshah, Dhan Guru Dhan Guru Pyar-e, Vaheguru Vaheguru Vaheguru.*"

Sada Kaur recited more *Gurbani* with much fervour before sitting down and reflecting on what she had just experienced. Her face was glowing, and a renewed sense of duty was coupled with a spirit of invincibility. As the realization of the encounter she had just experienced began to pass, she was instantly hit with another deeply moving and empowering realization. The *kirpan* that was lying by her side was now completely unsheathed, sparkling back at her brighter than a bolt of lightning.

Sada Kaur quickly picked up the *kirpan*, placed the hilt in her hand, and bowed her head towards the blade. She recited Guru Gobind Singh's *Bir Ras Bani* and then stood up from where she was sitting. She felt as light as a flower, but the blood in her veins seemed to be pumping more powerfully. Her eyes glistened with new sparkle, and her soul filled with pure fearlessness.

Sada Kaur thought to herself, *Akal Purakh has blessed me. With their support, I will surely regain my lost territory and build a strong Khalsa Raj. Now I must move quickly and waste no time in this mission.*

Looking at her own arms and legs, feeling the power that resonated throughout her entire being, Sada Kaur continued her meditation on the Supreme Force. *Akal Purakh, I say this with no sense of ego or individuality, but I vow to work only for the betterment of all for the rest of my life. I shall stand against the oppressor, uphold faith and the sovereignty of the Khalsa Panth. I will stand for the downtrodden and lift them up. I will not put down my sword until the Khalsa captures power in the name of the Guru. The stars in the sky bear witness to this pledge of mine; I shall not stop until I create a Raj worthy of the sacrifices made by our great ancestors. Those who fought alongside the Guru, and those who went on to conquer Sirhind, withstanding the oppression of the blood-thirsty rulers. I shall bring the oppressor to his knees. I am a servant of your Panth.*

As the first rays of sunshine began to pour in over the horizon in the east, Sada Kaur's attention shifted to the *Granthi*, who could be heard reciting *Asa Di Var*. Sada Kaur eased herself back into the frequency of the *Shabad*. Her mind was attuned to the Guru's words, especially the lines that speak of the Creator who makes gods out of mere mortals. Those lines were reverberating around her entire being. She repeated the *Shabad* to herself many times. In a state of complete bliss, Sada Kaur felt liberated; her conscious firmly focused on the sweet melody of the Guru's word.

# 8.

Sada Kaur was sat watching the sunrise, completely mesmerised by its beauty. She was still reflecting on the encounter from earlier that morning. The sun's rays appeared more attractive than ever before, almost as if they were sending a new message to her. The light was reaching out and saying, *Sada Kaur it's time to leave the comforts of the palace and jump on your horse again; the battlefield awaits you. It is now time to fight for the sacred land of the five rivers. The cold, mountainous region of the Himalayas is calling out for you. The Satluj and Attock rivers are calling your name. The peoples of Kashmir, Khyber, and Haripur are waiting for your feet to touch their land.*

Sada Kaur stood up and came down from her balcony, heading straight to her room. She changed clothes and headed towards the door, where Rami stood waiting. Upon seeing her, Sada Kaur said, "Rami, please immediately find and bring both Dal Singh and Secretary Ram Chand. Please be quick."

Rami nodded and swiftly left to find the two. Sada Kaur headed towards her *divan khana,* where she would discuss and deliberate on all important matters. What Sada Kaur had in mind that day was of utmost importance.

Rami stepped outside and headed towards the military barracks, where Dal Singh was stationed. Upon entering she noticed that Ram Chand was also there, so she informed them of Sada Kaur's request. They both immediately stopped what they were doing and followed Rami back to the *divan khana,* located in the centre of the palace.

As Rami stood guard outside the room, both Dal Singh and Ram Chand entered to see Sada Kaur stood against the wooden desk at the far end of the room in front of the large window overlooking the garden. In her right hand, she toyed with her unsheathed sword. This was the same sword that Gurbaksh Singh had fought with at the battle of Achal. As Sada Kaur moved the kirpan, she was reciting a passage from Chandi Charitt, Ukat Bilas:

**"When Chandi appeared with her sword in the battlefield, none of the demons could stand her rage.**
**She killed and destroyed them all.**
**Who can then wage a war without their king?**
**The enemies trembled with fear in their hearts;**
**they abandoned the pride of their heroism.**
**Then the demons, leaving the battlefield,**
**ran away like good qualities from avarice".**

After reciting the last line, Sada Kaur called out a powerful *Fateh,* battle cry, which Dal Singh and Ram Chand both repeated in equal measures. Sada Kaur motioned them in and asked them to take a seat.

"I have called you both here this morning to find out the expanse of the Misl's territory and for a breakdown on the current revenues. Which towns and cities upon the sacred land of the five rivers fall under our dominion? What is the current size of our army?" asked Sada Kaur.

Ram Chand was about fifty years old. He was well versed in Persian, Gurmukhi, and Hindi, which was why he was the Misl's secretary. He was a good writer and accountant, taking pride in his work. He answered each of the questions with great clarity. On the question related to the army, he said, "During the time of Vadde Sarkar (Jai Singh) there were 7000 soldiers, but following the martyrdom of Chotte Sarkar (Gurbaksh Singh) this number came down. At present, there are approximately 2500 soldiers in our army. While the numbers have decreased, I can say each soldier is strong, brave, and loyal to the Misl. They can be fully trusted to serve the Misl to the best of their ability."

Upon hearing this, Sada Kaur said, "Very well; this number of soldiers is sufficient. Dal Singh, ready the forces. First, we shall march on Kadia, followed by Kalanaur,

Sujanpur, and Pathankot, and our eventual victory will be over Kangra."

Whilst Ram Chand was good at what he did, he did not understand the art of war. Whenever there was any military movement, he remained locked inside his office. Lowering his eyes, he said, "Sarkar, we are grossly outnumbered. They have great strength in numbers. We should not rush into this; rather, we should wait and build up our fighting force. We have just lost two great leaders, and we're vulnerable to further attacks. I don't think it would be wise to launch an attack now; we could …" Ram Chand stopped mid-sentence as he looked up at Sada Kaur.

As a true *Sant-Sipahi*, saintly-warrior, Sada Kaur was ever-ready for war. Placing her hand on the hilt of her sword, Sada Kaur turned to Ram Chand, "Dear Secretary," she started.

"Hanji, Sarkar," replied Ram Chand.

"I am not concerned with how well, or ill-equipped, the enemy may be. Your job is to keep account of the books and deal with administrative matters. While I respect and appreciate the work you do, I did not ask you for advice on warfare. As commander-in-chief, that is my decision to make, and I say we wage war in order to take back our Raj!"

Ram Chand was unable to look Sada Kaur in the face. Upon hearing her words, his body was shaking from head to toe. The pen that he usually kept upon his right ear fell to the floor. This was the first time he had been called into to meet Sada Kaur since Jai Singh's passing, and he didn't want it to be the last. Without saying a word, he nodded and picked up his pen.

Sada Kaur then turned to Dal Singh and said, "Please assemble all of our soldiers and bring them into the open courtyard. I wish to inspect them. Gather our tents and items for camp, including our weapons, essentials, and enough food for the whole unit. We will leave for Kadia tomorrow morning. Those who underestimate me and deem me to be a weak leader will soon feel the full force of a daughter of Guru Gobind Singh!"

Dal Singh, a *jujharoo* fighter, was ever-ready for battle. He smiled and turned to head towards the door. As he did so, Rami re-appeared and said, "Forgive me, Sarkar, but somebody is here to see you. A young woman, who has said her name is Desa. We have asked her why she wants to see you; however, she is insistent on speaking with you and only you. She says she is from Pathankot."

"I will ask her to wait while you have your breakfast, Sarkar," continued Rami.

Sada Kaur thought for a moment and then spoke, "No, I will eat later. Please send the woman through immediately; I wish to hear why she is so eager to see me. It could be that she needs something, or her life could be in danger!"

"As you wish," replied Rami, before leaving the *divan khana* to bring Desa.

In the meantime, Sada Kaur asked Ram Chand some further questions about the treasury and finances of the Misl. The situation of the farmers and the harvest were also spoken about. This discussion between Sada Kaur and her secretary went on for about fifteen minutes.

Desa was a twenty-year-old woman. She had a strong frame, big cat-like eyes, rosy red cheeks, and thick black hair. She walked tall and was carrying her own sword as she followed Rami to the *divan khana*. On that day, she held her *chuni* over her face, as was the custom in those days, which draped down the back of her tall body.

As Desa entered the *divan khana*, Sada Kaur was pleasantly surprised to see another strong woman carrying a sword. Upon seeing Sada Kaur, Desa's strong and sturdy exterior bowed in respect, and then tears began to roll down her face. Without warning, she burst out, "Rani ji, please! Please save them. Their lives are in danger." Desa then fell at Sada Kaur's feet.

"In the name of God, please act quickly; otherwise, they will be killed," Desa sobbed on the ground.

"Whose life is in danger? Who will be killed? Please explain the whole situation, slowly and truthfully," replied Sada Kaur, as she picked Desa up by the arms.

"It does not suit you, such a strong woman, crying at my feet. Please tell me what happened!" continued Sada Kaur.

"His name is Varyam Singh," said Desa.

"He is from the village of Dharmuvala. He was a soldier in the army and used to live in the fort of Pathankot. He was known as Faujdar," explained Desa.

Sada Kaur continued to listen as Desa explained further.

"Following the martyrdom of the king, the ruler of Kangra, Sansar Chand, attacked the fort of Pathankot, and Varyam Singh was taken prisoner, along with ten others who were with him. They have been beaten in custody; I have tried many times to try and break them out but have not been able to get past their guards, who patrol the walls all day and all night."

"Who is he to you?" asked Sada Kaur.

"He is my ..." Desa stopped in her tracks, "what can I say ..."

"Are you two married?" Sensing Desa was hesitant to explain her relationship with Varyam Singh, Sada Kaur asked a leading question.

"No, Rani ji, I am not married."

"Are you engaged to this man; is he your fiancé?"

"Yes, we are engaged to marry."

"And what does he say? Why are they beating him?".

"My dear Rani, what they have told me worries me. Sansar Chand is a vile man. He is a dog, a crazy dog!"

Desa was now angry. The tears had stopped rolling, and her face was red with rage. Clenching her fist in the air, she continued, "If I ever get my hands on that man, I will break his bones ..."

Sada Kaur interrupted, "Please explain what he has done."

Desa asked for the men to leave the room, which Sada Kaur duly agreed to. She signalled Dal Singh and Ram Chand to leave the *divan khana*. When they had left, Desa looked up at Rami before turning to Sada Kaur and said,

"Rani ji, Sansar Chand came to Pathankot himself, and he asked Varyam Singh ..."

Sensing she was hesitating, Sada Kaur pressed her again, "What did he ask?"

"He gave them an option to leave the prison. The condition was dependent upon them bringing you to Sansar Chand," explained Desa.

"Why would he say this?" asked Sada Kaur.

"He is always speaking lustfully of your youthfulness and your beauty. However, when he spoke this way, Varyam Singh could not bear it. He swore at Sansar Chand and cursed him for thinking of you in that way. This is why he was taken away and is beaten daily."

Desa pleaded with Sada Kaur to help her rescue Varyam Singh and the others who were being held captive in the fort of Pathankot under Sansar Chand's orders.

"I see. Sansar Chand thinks he can woe me? He is going to regret even thinking, let alone speaking, of me in this way," said Sada Kaur.

Sada Kaur then turned towards the doors of the *divan khana* and clapped her hands. In an instant, both Dal Singh and Ram Chand re-entered the room. Sada Kaur then ordered, "Ready the army today. Before heading to Kandia, we shall be paying a visit to the fort of Pathankot. Leave a few soldiers here to stand guard in Batala. Sansar Chand's days as a ruler are now numbered. If he is desirous of seeing me, I will not disappoint him. I do not want to hear any excuse from you; ready the army right away."

Dal Singh and Ram Chand both nodded and hurriedly left the *divan khana* to prepare to leave the same day.

Sada Kaur turned to Rami, "Rami, take sister Desa with you. Make sure she is fed and then take out some appropriate clothes for her, and ready her a horse. From this day forward, she rides with us."

# 9.

The sound of the *Ranjit Nagara* being struck resounded out over the palace walls. The residents of Batala stopped what they were doing and turned their attention to the sound of the battle drum.

"Why is the *Ranjit Nagara* being struck?"

"I have no idea."

"Do you think it's a warning against an impending invasion?"

"There has been no message from the palace or the army to warn us of that."

The locals became anxious over why the war drum was reverberating from inside the palace walls. Many of the town's workers, including the carpenters, farmers, potters, jewellers, and ironsmiths, stopped what they were doing and headed outside to see if there was an official envoy from the palace. Some of the eager youth ran towards the palace.

"From which direction is the attack coming?" shouted one.

"I am prepared to join in with the battle; I too shall stand with our army and defend the dominion of our Misl," shouted another.

Alas, the gates of the palace walls sprung open. The locals realised they were not expecting an attack; rather, the Kanaiya Misl was preparing to leave for an attack. Upon seeing the army march out of the gates, many brave youths ran home and picked up their father's and grandfather's weapons and told them they were going with the army to wage war. Many women and *Singhnia* assembled together and formed a *jatha* to join the army. Those who were unable to leave with the marching army ran to their homes' rooftops and saw the spectacle from high vantage points.

Sada Kaur, who had witnessed her husband and father-in-law leave the palace to wage battle, was feeling proud. At the front of the march, she sat on her horse, Vayu, fully armed from head to toe in the best weapons the Misl had in its combatant arsenal. Beside her rode Dal Singh, Rami, and Desa, followed by battle-hardened, *tyar-bar-tyar* Singhs and *Singhnia*.

Some of the womenfolk who stood on the rooftops of their homes were completely in awe of Sada Kaur and began to sing her praises.

"This queen of ours is definitely a courageous goddess incarnate."

"She is the form of Durga!"

"She will collect the bones of her enemies; she will seek revenge for the king's spilt blood."

As Sada Kaur led the march out of the *haveli*, Vayu, a top breed horse from Kandhar, who had been a loyal companion of Sada Kaur's for many years, was galloping in unison with the wind.

Desa rode alongside Rami, just behind Sada Kaur. She, too, was in fierce battle gear. The three appeared like lionesses that led the pack during a hunt, with the lions close behind. In Desa's mind, she was focused entirely on freeing Varyam Singh and punishing Sansar Chand for his immoral ways.

Elsewhere warriors such as Dal Singh, Baghel Singh, Panj-Hatha Singh, and Nihaal Singh were present in the convoy that rode out of the town. Moments before, Sada Kaur had stood them all in the courtyard, "My brave and trusted soldiers, you are all like brothers and sisters to me. Remember, we are not going to loot or plunder any town.

I am leading you to recapture our land, but we shall remain true to the Khalsa way. Those who stand in our way should be convinced in line with Sikh tradition. I will lead us from the front. First, we shall march on Pathankot because that is where some of our brethren have been held captive, and we must free them first."

Listening to these words, various contingents within the army began to shout, *Bole So Nihaal, Sat Sri Akal*. The sound of *Jakaray,* battle cries, could be heard shattering against the sky.

"Our job is to establish *Khalsa Raj* over the pure and sacred land of the five rivers. Like those who came before me, I promise to look after you and reward you if you vow to stand with me and help the Misl regain its lost territory today," roared Sada Kaur.

"Once we free our brothers in Pathankot, then we shall march towards Sandar Chand. I hear he is waiting for me, and we don't want to keep him waiting, do we Singho?"

Again, the army of Singhs erupted with battle cries, wide-eyed and raring to pounce like lions before the kill. In unison, the army could be heard shouting back their words of commitment to the cause. While the *Ranjit Nagara* was struck, the *narsingha* too was brought out as they left the palace.

As Sada Kaur tightened her grip on the reins and harnessed more speed from Vayu, her mind was totally focused on the tasks before her. As she thought about the victory, her mind turned to what Desa had told her a couple of hours ago in the *divan khana.*

*Sansar Chand wants to make you his own.* At that moment, Sada Kaur imagined the loving face of her brave husband, and she thought, *I will never take another for my husband. This Sansar Chand will pay for his actions and his dirty thoughts. If he so much as looks towards me in that way, I'll take his eyes in one move. In remembrance of my beloved husband shall I perform the true sati of my faith in us. Come on, Vayu, quicker! Get me to Pathankot as quick as you can!*

With these thoughts, Sada Kaur felt a sudden surge of energy run through her body, and she struck her ankle against Vayu, who immediately picked up speed. The horses of Dal Singh, Desa, and Rami too picked up speed. The rest of the cavalry seemed to momentarily slow down before making up ground on their glorious leader at the front of the pack.

There were approximately two thousand horses behind Sada Kaur, and her own horse was now galloping at top speed. On route to Pathankot, they passed many towns, gardens, and fields, but Sada Kaur did not stop once. As they left the dominion of their own jurisdiction, Vayu's hooves crossed into the territory Sansar Chand had laid claim to. There was an outpost of Sansar Chand's in Sarhadi, which had a small number of soldiers stationed within it. When they saw the Kanaiya Misl horses marching towards them, they hurriedly prepared themselves, but their efforts were in vain. Sada Kaur led the charge, and within fifteen minutes, the entire outpost had been slayed. The locals were spared, the houses were not looted, and no women or children were harassed.

Sada Kaur summoned the town's chief and said, "From this moment forward, this town does not belong to Sansar Chand. It now falls under the care and protection of Batala. The Kanaiya Misl is now here to serve you."

The chief took one look at Sada Kaur's blood-drenched sword and happily pledged his and the entire town's allegiance to Sada Kaur. Nishaan Sahibs were raised across the town.

Some of the womenfolk were utterly shocked – never before had they seen a woman command such respect. They were empowered by what they saw.

"Look, sister, she too is a woman, but she fights amongst men," one of them said.

"She not only fights amongst men, sister, but look – she leads some of the fiercest looking warriors I have seen," replied the other.

Sada Kaur took the reins of Vayu again and gave him the signal. The loyal horse turned around and once again galloped forward, quickly picking up speed. Nobody was able to stop them. Many people stepped back and allowed the horses to ride right past them.

The high rising houses of Pathankot could now be seen. Sada Kaur thought, *they're not ready to stand against the riders of this Misl. With the grace of Kalgidhar Patshah Sahib Sri Guru Gobind Singh, we shall be victorious.*

The fort of Pathankot was heavily fortified by brave and strong warriors, many of whom hailed from the rugged terrains of the northern mountains. The watchman of the high tower saw the army marching towards the fort and immediately sent a message to the other guards. Their soldiers were briefed and deployed around the fort.

Sada Kaur's army took over the town with relative ease and soon found themselves stood on the fort's outskirts. The sun had set for the day, and the whole town was now engulfed in darkness. It was almost impossible to launch an attack, and they were still waiting for some of the cavalry to arrive. As any intelligent leader does, Sada Kaur consulted with her commanders and decided to set up camp. They would wait for the moon to appear before launching any attack.

Desa had an idea, "Rani ji, should I disguise myself and sneak into the fort? If I am not able to bring them out, at the very least, I could try to open the gates for you all."

"There are guards stationed everywhere, Desa," replied Sada Kaur.

"Desa is not afraid of any guards; with your blessings and the support of Vaheguru, I have every confidence in my ability," said Desa.

Sada Kaur pondered over the idea for a moment and then agreed to it but ordered Desa to take a handful of soldiers with her.

"There is no need, Rani ji, I shall go alone."

"No, this is an order, you either take soldiers with you, or you don't go at all. How do you plan on breaching their defence?"

"On the northern side of the fort, there is a sturdy ivy plant that grows up against the wall. We shall take that opening."

"Shall I come with you?"

"No, Rani ji! You will step foot into the fort with dignity alongside the army. Your life is very dear to us. As long as your servants are alive, there is no need to risk your life."

With that, Desa took five brave warriors with her and climbed up the ivy plant on the northern wall, and discreetly disappeared into the fort.

# 10.

In the south of Kangra, which is situated in modern-day Himachal Pradesh, there once stood a famous fort founded by the Katoch dynasty's chiefs. During the late eighteenth century, the owner of this fort was Raja Sansar Chand. It was a mighty great fort built on a small hilltop; however, in 1905, the fort was heavily damaged following a powerful earthquake. Today, only remnants of the fort stand, as most of it has perished away.

Sansar Chand was engrossed in *maya*. The greed of temporal power and status had enticed him to give up the ways of a worthy leader. He had colluded with Maha Singh and Jassa Singh Ramgharia and taken a large part of Jai Singh's territory. That victory had only served to heighten his ego and sense of superiority.

On that day, Sansar Chand was sitting in the comfort and luxury of his private quarters. He was young, powerful, drunk, and surrounded by half-naked women from the mountainous region who were dancing for his pleasure. He did not seem to have a care in the world, unaware of the situation unfolding around him. This was the calm before the storm that Sada Kaur was about to unleash upon his entire existence.

He ushered one of the paid dancers to pour him some more rum. As she picked up the bottle, he grabbed her hand and brought it to his mouth. Sitting back, he told her to pour the bottle straight into his mouth. He smiled as others he had forcefully taken from their homes continued to dance in front of him.

At that moment, the doors flung open, and one of Sansar Chand's servants came rushing in. Out of breath, she said, "Sarkar, your minister wishes to see you straight away. I don't know what the matter is, but he is in a worrisome state."

"The minister? My minister? He wants to see me now … well tell him I … I will come straight away."

Laughing, Sansar Chand slurred his words back to the servant. He moved his head from side to side. Hiccupping loudly, he stumbled to his feet.

The servant took the bottle of rum and told the dancers to leave. Sensing some degree of urgency, Sansar Chand managed to find his balance and slowly edged out of the doors and headed towards his minister's office.

As he neared the office of his minister, Hira Chand, accompanied by some servants, Sansar Chand mumbled,

"He wants to see me, straightaway?" and then, flinging the door open, he splurted out, "Hira Chand, I was attending to important royal business, what is it!"

Looking up at his drunk king, Hira Chand started, "Sarkar ..."

"What happened? Why have you spoiled my evening?" snapped back Sansar Chand, his eyes now bloodshot and red.

"Sarkar, Rani Sada Kaur is stood outside the fort, and there is a large army contingent with her. She has already taken over Pathankot and Nurpur. In both instances, she has secured the services of our soldiers. Darkness has befallen us now – before the next sunrise, they will launch an attack!"

Upon hearing this, Sansar Chand shook off a little of his drunkenness. Stepping towards Hira Chand, he asked, "Which Sada Kaur?"

Hira Chand replied, "The widow of Gurbaksh Singh of Batala, Sardar Jai Singh Kanaiya's daughter-in-law. Our man in the watchtower has informed us that she is leading the attack on horseback herself. They were able to take the fort of Pathankot with ease; our soldiers were unable to fight back, so surrendered their weapons. Varyam Singh was freed. At Nurpur, hundreds of our men were killed. The Sikh army has been mobilised all around the town."

Sansar Chand rubbed his eyes and appeared to shake off a little more of his drunkenness. He did not register what Hira Chand had said about Pathankot and Nurpur.

"Ah right, that Sada Kaur, the one whom I wanted to meet! The same Sada Kaur that my eyes have desired to see for some time, she is here!" Sansar Chand's mind took the news of Sada Kaur's arrival to mean something else.

"Sarkar! Please try to understand. This is serious; we need to prepare the fort against this imminent attack. Please snap out of it; this crazy talk will have us killed!"

Upon hearing this, Sansar Chand's eyes opened up, and he registered what his minister had been saying. Stumbling back, he immediately ordered the guards on duty to roll out the cannons and place them on the fort's walls. He ordered another set of guards to prepare the elephants and horses in readiness for the battle. As he was handing out his orders, one of the main commanders entered the minister's office and yelled, "They have taken over all of our outposts, they have even crossed Shahpur, and Sikh forces have taken up their positions along the river too. What should we do?"

"So, what? Assemble the troops, march out into the town, and face them head-on! After all, she is just a woman!!" cried back Sansar Chand.

"She is no ordinary woman; she is a woman on a mission to take this fort! We should consider all our options, including a diplomatic resolution," said the commander.

Upon hearing these words, Sansar Chand appeared to snap completely out of his drunken state. In an angry tone, he snapped back, "I will not enter into a diplomatic resolution with a woman. Go now! Fight, and die if you must. I don't want to hear anything else. Go now; I too shall be right behind you."

As the guards and commander marched out of the minister's office, Sansar Chand followed them - however, instead of readying himself for battle, he walked straight into the dancers' chambers and opened a new bottle of rum.

A couple of hours before sunrise, Sada Kaur decided to launch her attack on the town of Kangra. The force of two thousand with which she had left Batala now stood at approximately five thousand. The entire contingent deployed in Pathankot had aligned themselves with Sada Kaur. Her courage and bravery had won the locals' hearts, especially the youth who were inspired by her actions. The Singhs within her army saw Sada Kaur as a sister, mother, or daughter, and the same could be said of the Misl's *Singhnia* and how they perceived their leader.

Every soldier only had victory in their sights, which was down to the confidence Sada Kaur had instilled within them. Each one was vying to take Sansar Chand's head back to Batala as a trophy piece.

Within a matter of hours, Sada Kaur and the Kanaiya Misl had defeated Sansar Chand's men. The most resistance was shown by the contingent of troops with elephants, but it was not enough to stop the Sikhs from taking over the town of Kangra.

Inside the fort, having drunk himself to sleep, Sansar Chand had just awoken from his slumber. All of his main ministers and courtiers were trapped inside the fort with him. Outside, Sada Kaur stood like a mountain and roared, "I wish to arrest Sansar Chand. I want to see him alive. The whole of Kangra is now under my control. Give yourself up, Sansar Chand!"

There was no reply from within the fort. The doors remained tightly shut. Sada Kaur decided to send a letter.

*The Sada Kaur you were so eager to meet is standing outside your fort. Open the gates and come meet her. If you do not respond by sunset, we will attack the fort.*

She then tied the short letter to an arrow and masterfully fired it towards the fort's gates. The arrow pierced one of the guards, killing him instantly. One of the other guards saw the letter and immediately took it to his commander, who took it straight to Sansar Chand. When he read the letter, he began to shake. After much deliberation with his advisors, Sansar Chand decided to raise the white flag above the fort. He said he would open the gates and himself walk out to seek forgiveness from Sada Kaur.

Outside, two hours had passed when Sada Kaur and her army heard the gates of the fort open and saw the white flag of surrender waving in the wind. Upon hearing someone shout, "We surrender, let's come to an agreement," Sada Kaur summoned Dal Singh and ordered him to take a *jatha,* unit, of five Singhs to go and establish what they were suggesting.

As Dal Singh prepared the *jatha,* Sansar Chand's minister, Hira Chand, and the chief commander walked out of the gates and headed towards them. As they approached Sada Kaur, Hira Chand knelt down, greeted them with a *Fateh,* and declared that Sansar Chand was prepared to accept Sada Kaur as his sovereign, and with humility sought forgiveness for his actions.

Sada Kaur listened to his words and then lifted her head towards the fort, "Those kings and rulers who govern with greed and their own egos have created hell upon this heaven-like world created by Vaheguru. Through their self-centredness and manipulation, they have brought much misery upon this world. Before accepting any apology or oath of allegiance, I wish to hear from Sansar Chand. Tell him to come out and meet me in person."

# 11.

Sansar Chand sat on the ground in front of Sada Kaur. His head was down; unable to lift his gaze towards the towering warrior queen, he was in an utter heap of shame and humiliation. Defeated and embarrassed, he was just giving simple yes or no answers to Sada Kaur's line of questioning.

"I want to hear this from you. Speak up, man! Is it true that you are willing to accept me as your sovereign?" asked Sada Kaur in a commanding tone.

Sansar Chand remained quiet. He did not say a word to either accept or reject what Sada Kaur had said.

"I want to hear you speak!" roared Sada Kaur.

With his eyes fixated on the ground before him, Sansar Chand began to mumble some words:

"Sister, please … please forgive me, I …"

"Sansar Chand, I had heard you wanted to make me your own property. I heard you had plans to take on the Kanaiya Misl; to capture and occupy the region of Batala. Where are your grand threats now?"

"Sister, please take pity on me. I have made many mistakes," started Sansar Chand.

"Did you not know I am the daughter of Guru Gobind Singh, the King of kings? In the eyes of the world, I may be a widow, but they do not know of the rage that burns within me. They do not know of my faith in Vaheguru and my desire to secure *Khalsa Raj* over all of Panjab. Are you aware of the sin you have amassed with such lowly thoughts and actions?"

"I am the greatest sinner; I deserve all of the punishment I get," replied Sansar Chand remorsefully.

Sada Kaur paused for a moment, sensing some degree of sincerity to his words, and she asked whether he had a daughter.

"Yes, I do, she is only ten months old."

"Good. Now listen carefully. I do not have a son. I have one daughter, Mehtab Kaur, who will marry Ranjit Singh, the son of Maha Singh of Sukerchakia Misl. My condition is this. When your daughter comes of age, you must agree to marry her to Ranjit Singh, and if you have a second daughter, she too must marry Ranjit Singh. Do you accept these terms?"

Without hesitation, Sansar Chand looked up for the first time, and with a smile, said, "Yes, yes, of course, I would be honoured."

"Now the second condition. If you want to rule over Kangra and Juwala, you will not step foot towards Nurpur or any of the other territories that lead back to Batala. They now fall under the jurisdiction of the Kanaiya Misl."

"Yes, yes, I accept those conditions, Rani ji."

"I will slowly bring an end to these small kingships and create one Great Raj over Panjab. To assist me in this, are you prepared to send me your soldiers?" Sada Kaur shared her vision and posed a question to test Sansar Chand's newly-found loyalty.

"I will have four thousand of my most able and brave soldiers ready for your call. Whenever you command, I shall send them to you. If you need more, I will recruit more. I am fully in debt to your mercy, my Queen."

This was Sada Kaur's first big victory. She was able to win a key dominion, secure their allegiance to her Misl, and regain some of the territory they had lost. She remained in Kangra for eight days before returning to Batala. When they left, Sansar Chand bestowed many gifts, jewels, and pearls upon Sada Kaur and her army. The convoy left victorious, singing songs of joy and happiness as they returned to Batala.

As Sada Kaur rode back to Batala, she remembered all the stories her father had told her about the initial victories of the Misls. Individuals such as Jassa Singh Ahluwalia, the founder of Kapurthala State; Charat Singh, founder of Sukerchakia Misl; Jhanda Singh and Hari Singh of Bhangi

Misl; Sham Singh and Baghel Singh of Karoorsinghian Misl; Jassa Singh of Ramgharia Misl; and of course, Jai Singh of Kanaiya Misl. Empowered by the sovereignty of the Guru Khalsa Panth, they all carved out their own territories through sheer grit and determination.

While it had been almost thirty years since the Misls were formed, and some of the leaders had lost sight of the wider political mandate Guru Gobind Singh had given to the Khalsa, Sada Kaur was still inspired by their daring actions. Through inspirational and visionary leaders such as Nawab Kapur Singh, the Misls eventually took political power in Panjab. The *Nishan Sahibs* had also been raised above Delhi many times, and Sada Kaur knew she had a mammoth task of uniting Panjab again.

Since the original Misl leaders had either perished or wandered astray, there was a need for the Sikhs to reorganise and rebuild. The geopolitical landscape was changing due to foreign invasion from the far west, particularly from the British, who were annexing territory after territory in the south. Panjab was the last bastion, and Sada Kaur knew its independence was of key importance to the region. With Vayu galloping at top speed, she continued to ponder the task that lay ahead, planning and strategizing how she would make her next move to bring about a new era of Sikh rule in Panjab.

She also thought back to the vision she had witnessed a few days ago and remembered the sacrifices of the Guru's own cousins who had fought so valiantly in the Battle of

Bhangani. She remembered their determination to continue marching forward despite the large number of enemy troops standing in front of them. Sada Kaur thought this victory of hers was important, but she knew she must remain focused; there were many more battles to come.

As Vayu approached the River Beas, Sada left a deployment of forces at the fort of Pathankot and Dina Nagar to handle matters on her behalf. On the final stretch down to Batala, Sada Kaur continued to ponder over the next course of action.

*Many people talk of bringing change. Perhaps Sansar Chand once thought he could bring change too, but as he amassed a little power, he lost his way. Engrossed in the pleasure of worldly comforts, his mind became a slave to lust, greed, and attachment. You cannot allow yourself to fall into that trap, Sada Kaur! The Guru has provided everything. Stay strong. Stay connected to the frequency of the Shabad, and allow the Will of Vaheguru to lead us to victory.*

Sada Kaur took the victory over Kangra as her very own Battle of Bhangani; while it was a milestone victory, she had to build from this. The Guru went on to wage many further battles in order to advance the Khalsa Panth and uphold Sikh principles of equality, liberty, and freedom for all. Through waging war against oppression and tyranny, the Guru endured much hardship, lost the city of Anandpur Sahib, and with it, countless priceless handwritten manuscripts and treasures, his four sons, and his mother. Thousands of his Khalsa also perished, but he remained steadfast. It was due to the Guru's resilience and determination to create a better world that he raised up Banda Singh, who desecrated all systems of oppression, eventually establishing the Khalsa Republic.

*As rulers of individual territories over Panjab we've experienced sovereignty but entangled ourselves in meaningless battles for supremacy. The political landscape is changing, and we must now stand under one Nishaan Sahib and manifest the glorious governance of Khalsa Raj. Understand Sada Kaur, this path will not be easy. This path is thinner than a strand of hair and sharper than a sword's edge. Be prepared to endure hardship; don't lose sight of the Panthic Nishana, the overall aim, and above all, be prepared to sacrifice your possessions, your mind, and your body in battle.*

Absorbed in such thoughts, Sada Kaur arrived back in Batala. The month of Vaisakhi was fast approaching. The new harvest in the fields of Panjab was joyfully swaying with the gentle wind. Many Sikhs across Panjab were travelling towards Sri Harmandir Sahib, *Amrit*sar, to mark the annual celebrations. Under the rule of Sada Kaur, Batala, too, was full of joy and laughter.

To mark her first victory and honour the celebrations of the month of *Vaisakhi,* Sada Kaur arranged a large *mela.* Sports and wrestling competitions were held, *kabaddi, sochi, Gurbani Kirtan Darbars,* and *Akhand Paths* were also held. The courageous and brave warriors of the Kanaiya Misl were awarded for their fighting prowess. The royal courts were brightly decorated, and at night, the lights could be seen for miles. A large *Langar* was prepared and *Prashad,* sacred food, was handed out. Thousands took part to join in with the celebrations.

# 12.

Just like night arrives after the day has passed, we too must endure the darker moments that follow days of joy and happiness. Such is life; a constant balance between the two states of being, intertwined like the thorns sitting within the rose bushes. We must take the bad with the good as we find our way across the world.

A day after the happiness and laughter of the *Vaisakhi* gathering and *mela,* a messenger travelled to Batala from Gujranwala. As he approached the palace gates in the early hours of the night, he handed a message to the guards on duty:

"Rani Sada Kaur should be notified immediately. Maha Singh, head of the Sukerchakia Misl, has been taken ill, and the doctors have said he does not have many days left. Rani Sada Kaur must travel to Gujranwala immediately."

Sada Kaur had set firm ground rules regarding the exchange of foreign or external communications. She had told her ministers, courtiers, and servants that no matter what the news, and no matter what she was doing, any news should be brought to her immediately and without delay.

The message found its way to Rami, who took it straight to Sada Kaur, "Sarkar, we have just received news regarding Maha Singh of Gujranwala. He has been taken ill and is having trouble breathing. You have been requested to meet him immediately."

Sada Kaur immediately stood up and ordered Rami to prepare the horses. She asked for Desa and fifteen or so others to join them for the journey to Gujranwala. Dal Singh was to remain in Batala and take charge of matters in her absence. Sada Kaur also told Rami to see that their guest was offered food and a place to rest before he left.

The convoy was readied within an hour, and they left Batala for Gujranwala, with Dal Singh remaining behind to deputise. The horses galloped north during *Amrit Vela,* passing through many towns. The sound of the horses' hooves awoke many locals. They soon crossed the River Ravi and, within a short while, arrived in Gujranwala. The mist of early Visakh was covering the ground. There was an air of emptiness and sense of grief throughout the city, a stark contrast to the festive spirit that had captivated Batala the day before.

Sada Kaur arrived at the *haveli* of Maha Singh, dismounted her horse, and made her way straight to the room where Maha Singh was lying with the doctors beside him. The room was full of close family, all of whom were sitting quietly, or praying for the speedy recovery of their king.

"Bhenji, you made it! Thank you for coming," Maha Singh himself welcomed Sada Kaur, "I wanted to see you before my body gave up on me, but apologies for asking you to travel at such short notice."

Sada Kaur reassured Maha Singh it was no trouble at all.

"Such is the Will of Vaheguru. My father passed away when I was ten years old, and today my Ranjit Singh too is ten years old. I am fearful now my son will become an orphan at such a young age, with no one to guide him in the art of politics and governance. He will be vulnerable to the clutches of those who wish to bring the Sukerchakia Misl down. I have one request to you, bhenji."

Sada Kaur once again reassured Maha Singh to remain confident in the support and protection of Vaheguru. She knelt beside him, taking his hand, and said, "Yes, please tell me. I am ready to give you my word."

"My Ranjit Singh. From this day forward, I hand him over to you. You are to care for him and raise him as your own. Until he comes of age, I ask you to advise the Sukerchakia Misl. I have full faith you will strengthen the Misl to the best of your ability."

"I am honoured. I vow to look after Ranjit Singh as my own son. Your son will go on to establish one of the most glorious Sikh kingdoms across all of Panjab."

At that moment, young Ranjit Singh was sat close by his father's bed. Even at a young age, he appeared to be handling the situation well. The small scars around his left eye socket were minute but visible. Despite losing his eye to smallpox during infancy, he was a handsome young boy.

Ranjit Singh's mother, Raj Kaur, was also sitting next to her husband, holding his arm. She was beside herself and couldn't stop the tears that were rolling down her face. Her husband was still young, at thirty-five years of age. Having heard many great stories about Rani Sada Kaur, Raj Kaur sat and listened to every word she had said since arriving. In truth, Raj Kaur had been a little apprehensive when Maha Singh had made the request. She knew how her husband was responsible for the death of Sada Kaur's own husband, and despite learning of her heroic deeds since the Battle of Achal, Raj Kaur was not sure how Sada Kaur would take to what Maha Singh had to say.

However, from the moment Sada Kaur walked through the door, Raj Kaur knew she had no reason to worry. She had never met another woman like Sada Kaur, whose aura and presence took command over the whole room. As she listened to further exchanges between her husband and

Sada Kaur, feeling at ease and inspired by the leader of the Kanaiya Misl, a familiar voice also spoke up, "*Pita ji*, do not worry about the Misl. There is much strength and power in our Misl. Your Ranjit Singh will win many battles in the name of *Khalsa Raj*. Both of my mothers will protect and support me. With Vaheguru's grace, I will defeat all the enemies." Ranjit Singh stood up as he spoke.

Upon hearing his son speak in such a brave manner, Maha Singh's mind was put at ease. He was reminded of the similar words he had spoken at his own father's passing in 1770. He had many fond memories of his father, Charat Singh, who would take time to narrate the adventures of his own father, Maha Singh's grandfather, Nodh Singh. Nodh Singh had joined Nawab Kapur Singh's Fyzulpuria Misl during the time of Ahmed Shah Abdali's first invasion. As Nodh Singh and others of the Misl defended Panjab against the Afghani invaders, they laid siege to the loot and treasures that the invaders had amassed, thus enriching their own personal wealth. Nodh Singh became known as the leader of Sukerchak because that was where he had gathered his riches.

In 1747, Nodh Singh encountered another force of Afghani invaders and suffered a gunshot to the head. While the bullet did not take his life, it was a debilitating blow, and the final five years of his life were spent without interfering much in political affairs. The leadership of

Sukerchakia Misl eventually came to rest on Charat Singh's shoulders, who slowly amassed influential control over the Gujranwala area. He had many encounters with the marauding Afghan invaders but continued to build strong alliances with other kings, especially in Jammu.

Maha Singh was overcome with pride, and tears of joy began to flow down his face as he thought of his forefathers. Pointing to his sword and shield, Maha Singh said, "*Shabash putt,* well done, son.

"I too was only ten years old when my father passed. I picked up his sword and shield and vowed to lead the Sukerchakia Misl to the best of my ability. Your grandfather's sword has served me well. It has seen many a battlefield. For over twenty years, it has protected me and this Misl. Now, I hand this over to you. You must wield it to deliver justice, righteousness, and a rule that serves the welfare of everyone. Listen to Sada Kaur; she will guide and train you. Always start every task with an *Ardas,* so that Guru and *Akal Purakh* may lead you to victory."

Maha Singh's trust in Sada Kaur was, in many ways, history repeating itself. Before his father Charat Singh had died, he had turned to Jai Singh Kanaiya for assistance too. Sensing Maha Singh was too young to fulfil the duty of Misl chief, Charat Singh had relied on an old friend to assist. Before their recent clashes, the two Misls, under the stewardships of Jai Singh and Maha, had fought many battles together, including the famous march on Rassulnagar, which was later renamed Ramnagar. This was the attack in which Maha Singh and Jai Singh, with a six thousand strong contingent, had defeated Pir Mohamed of the Chatta Tribe and regained the *zamzama* gun, claiming it as the property of the Khalsa. The famous gun said to have been one of the longest ever made in South Asia, went on to be used by Sikh forces throughout the early nineteenth century.

Sada Kaur watched as young Ranjit Singh continued to listen attentively to his father's words of wisdom. She sensed a great love and closeness between father and son, but also a pain in Maha Singh's words at the prospect of leaving his son to fend for himself at such a young age. Despite the fact that Maha Singh had played a damning role in her own husband's death, she knew this was the moment to go beyond the personal inter-Misl grievances. She saw the bigger picture, the pressing matter of revitalising Sikh political power in Panjab to secure a strong dominion and defend against new foreign invaders.

As she watched father and son speak, the doctors administered further medicine to Maha Singh. Despite the medicine and everyone's well-wishes, Maha Singh's health soon took a turn for the worse.

Sada Kaur, Raj Kaur, Ranjit Singh, the doctors, and *Granthis* were all in the room. As Maha Singh lost consciousness, the doctor held his arm with a finger on his pulse. After a few minutes, he dropped his head and slowly placed Maha Singh's arms across his chest. The soul had left the body for its next journey.

There was great mourning across Gujranwala and other districts where Maha Singh was loved. Prayers were recited in the Gurdwara, Mandirs, and Mosques as people of all backgrounds were deeply saddened with his passing.

# 13.

Following Maha Singh's death, Ranjit Singh was declared leader of the Sukerchakia Misl. At that time, Divan Lakhpat Rai was responsible for overseeing the Misl's finances. Raj Kaur, although strong of mind and politically astute, felt she needed to do more to protect her son and the Misl.

One day, she approached Sada Kaur and said, "Bhenji, you must guide this Misl too. There are many other Sardars and Misls who want to bring us down. The Bhangis of Gujrat and Lahore are very bitter and jealous of what we have achieved. We must do everything in our power to protect young Ranjit Singh."

"Whosoever even dares to look at Ranjit Singh with bad intentions, I will remove their eyes. There is no need to worry; I am here with you, ever ready to protect the Sukerchakia Misl and Ranjit Singh. I have a duty towards both the Kaniaya and Sukerchakia Misl. We will ensure Ranjit Singh is crowned ruler over all of Panjab, with the support and blessings of Vaheguru." Sada Kaur offered much assurance to Raj Kaur.

"I intend to return to Batala for a month to take care of some matters; however, I will be back. I plan to uproot the small Misls in Sujanpuria, Mukeria, and Hoshiarpur, who are still opposing us."

Raj Kaur and Sada Kaur held further discourse on the best course of action needed to ensure that the grand plan of crowning Ranjit Singh ruler over all of Panjab would come to fruition. They talked for many hours into the evening. There was a new dawn on the horizon, and this time the strong-willed women of the Sikh Panth were the architects of a new Panjab.

Ranjit Singh had the support of Raj Kaur, Sada Kaur, and his minister Lakhpat Rai. In the immediate aftermath following Maha Singh's death, he was eager to continue his horse riding and hunting. Despite Sada Kaur's best efforts, he did not pay attention to formal study, choosing instead to spend his days on horseback with various members of the Sukerchakia army.

As Ranjit Singh played and enjoyed all the luxuries of being the chief, Lakhpat Rai managed the administrative affairs of the Misl, while Raj Kaur supported him. Sada Kaur was busy building the armies of both Kanaiya Misl and the Sukerchakia Misl, with the long-term aim of paving the way for Ranjit Singh's future conquests. She jostled for power within the Majha region before turning her attention to the Bhangis, who themselves had lost prominent leaders, but nevertheless maintained influential control over Lahore. This was significant because Panjab could not be unified without first taking Lahore.

Within a year following Maha Singh's death, Sada Kaur had taken over smaller Misls. Over the next few years, her fighting force continued to increase as she acquired more horses and weapons for both the Kanaiya and Sukerchakia Misls. In the mid-1790s, she was one of the most feared military generals across all of Panjab.

When she was not leading a charge to expand her territory, Sada Kaur would take Ranjit Singh on hunting and training expeditions. While the Sukerchakia Misl commanders were capable and highly skilled fighters, there were not many as daring and courageous as Sada Kaur.

It was the early summer months of 1794. Ranjit Singh, now fourteen-years-old, had accompanied Sada Kaur, Dal Singh, Rami, Desa, Varyam Singh, and a handful of others out on a hunting expedition. They rode out approximately fifty kilometres east towards the Beas River. An eager Ranjit Singh was galloping beside Sada Kaur at the front.

"Mata ji, can you tell me the story of Guru Hargobind Sahib and the royal hawk?"

Sada Kaur turned and smiled. She had first narrated this story to Ranjit Singh a couple of years back when he had come to learn *Shastar Vidhia* in Batala. She remembered his excitement at learning about the context to Guru Sahib's first battle, so she reined in Vayu, her trusty companion, and they slowed down the gallop.

"The year was 1629, and Guru Hargobind Sahib was out on a hunting expedition with his Sikhs. As it so happened, Shah Jahan, who had taken over as king of the Mughal empire after Jahangir, was also out hunting with his soldiers in the same area as the Guru.

"During his reign, Shah Jahan was frequently told about the Guru's political activity and the threat it posed to their own political ambitions. The establishment of *Akal Takht*, the Immortal Throne, in *Amrit*sar, by the Guru, had sent shockwaves throughout the Mughal echelons of power. It was a clear indication of the Guru's political and military mobilisation. He had amassed a fighting force too ..."

"The *Akal Sena*, the Immortal Army," shouted back Ranjit.

"Yes, the *Akal Sena*, a few members of whom were with the Guru during this hunting expedition. As they started their hunt, the Sikhs saw that the emperor's hawk, a rare white species from Persia, would pick up its prey and inflict a long and torturous death upon it, sometimes flinging the poor animal into the air, and other times throwing it to the ground. The Guru's Sikhs, who were taught to kill with one blow, could not bear to see the animal suffer, so they set the Guru's hawk upon the emperor's. Within a few seconds, the emperor's hawk was brought down by the Guru's hawk and instantly killed."

Ranjit Singh listened with great interest as Sada Kaur narrated the famous episode.

"News of the Sikhs taking the emperor's hawk soon reached Shah Jahan. His officials shouted, '*baaz nu hath paia ne, kal taj nu paunge,*' today they have taken your hawk, tomorrow they will reach for your throne.

"This was the pretext behind Guru Hargobind Sahib's first battle with Shah Jahan, who decided to launch a full-scale military attack on the Guru while he was stationed at the Fort of Lohgarh."

"Mata ji, who led the attack on Guru Sahib?" asked Ranjit.

"Shah Jahan had deputised Mukhlis Khan along with an army of approximately seven thousand soldiers to attack Lohgarh during the night. The *Akal Sena* was able to wade off the initial attack. Before sunrise, Guru Sahib had ordered for Guru Granth Sahib to be taken to Kartarpur, and Bibi Viro, their daughter, who was due to marry soon, was also safely taken out of the fort.

"As the sun rose, Guru Hargobind Sahib prepared the *Akal Sena,* reminding them of their duty to oppose oppressive forces. The Sikhs were heard singing the Guru's glory and remained in high spirits in readiness for the second attack, which they sensed was imminent. But Guru Sahib had other ideas. Riding out onto the battlefield, Guru Sahib fired an arrow that struck Mukhlis Khan's horse, which instantly fell to the ground. Guru Sahib then challenged Mukhlis Khan to a duel and allowed him to strike the first blow. In a fit of anger, Mukhlis Khan swung his sword, but Guru Sahib blocked his strike with his shield. The second strike was also blocked. As Mukhlis Khan prepared to strike a third time, Guru Sahib moved his *kirpan* so fast and with so much power that it sliced Mukhlis Khan's head straight off his body."

"Vaheguru! *Akal hi Akal*!" shouted Ranjit Singh.

"Guru Sahib then performed the final rites of the thirteen martyrs who fell in that battle; Bhai Nand ji, Bhai Jeth ji, Bhai Rina ji, Bhai Tota ji, Bhai Tiloka, Bhai Saidas, Bhai Khera, Bhai Bhagtu, Bhai Aninta, Bhai Nihalu, Bhai Takhtu, Bhai Mohan and Bhai Gopal ji."

As Sada Kaur spoke out the names, Dal Singh let out a powerful *Jakara,* which everyone answered. Spirits were high amongst the riders as they reached the banks of the Beas.

"Mata ji, how many battles did Guru Hargobind Sahib wage with the Mughals?" asked Ranjit.

"Five, son, and the Guru was victorious in all of them. We have been waging wars on oppressive rulers ever since. It is our duty as Sikhs of the Guru always to defend the weak and further the Khalsa Panth. This is why we train and come out on hunting expeditions to be ready for any strike. *Gurbani* nourishes our soul, and these weapons protect us. Without these weapons, we cannot fight the oppressors or further the Guru's objective of establishing *Khalsa Raj*. Without Raj, there is no control over *Dharam*, and without *Dharam,* everyone is lost. No one will give you Raj; whosoever wants it, takes it by force. But remember, son, as a ruler, you must always work for the welfare of all, and keep the Guru's teachings in mind."

Following Maha Singh's death, as Sada Kaur raised and nurtured Ranjit Singh, training him in *Shastar Vidhia,* horse riding, and allowing him to accompany her on hunting trips, she narrated many inspirational stories to him in this manner. They taught him the importance of standing for the righteous cause, no matter what the risk to his own life, as well as Sikh values of compassion, humility, and welfare for all.

While Ranjit Singh was himself illiterate, he always took time to learn about his own history as well as the histories of different world cultures and peoples by listening to others. The knowledge and understanding he gained from Sada Kaur's tutelage helped form his understanding of Sikh history more than anyone else.

Sikh history is littered with empowering stories about self-determination and sheer will overcoming unsurmountable odds in the face of their adversaries. In addition to the accounts of Guru Hargobind Sahib's battles, Sada Kaur would also narrate the battles of Guru Gobind Singh, talking about how they defended Anandpur Sahib and other sovereign Sikh territories, which was established by the Gurus. Banda Singh Bahadur's campaigns, and the aftermath which led to the eventual rise of Nawab Kapur Singh and the formation of the Misls, served as a constant reminder, to both Sada Kaur and Ranjit Singh, of their Panthic duty and responsibility to actualise the Guru's sovereignty.

Sada Kaur was a constant guide and role model for almost a decade, shaping and influencing Ranjit Singh's political ambitions. In 1795, Raj Kaur arranged Ranjit Singh's marriage to Datar Kaur, sister of Sardar Gian Singh Satghar; this marriage had been solemnised during his childhood.

A year later in 1796, Sada Kaur and Raj Kaur agreed to arrange the long-awaited wedding of Ranjit Singh and Mehtab Kaur. The wedding was held with great splendour and grandeur; no expenses were spared. The streets of

Batala and Gujranawala were decorated with bright lights, and thousands upon thousands lined the streets as Ranjit Singh's wedding party arrived in Batala.

Drums were played. Candles were lit at night. During *Amrit Vela, Asa-Di-Var* was recited, and a *Kirtan Darbar* was held before their *Anand Karaj* took place the following morning. After three days of celebrations in Batala, the newlyweds travelled home to Gujranwala.

# 14.

The country of Panjab, and the wider region of South Asia as it was prior to the creation of the Indian state, was a beautiful land, with a rich array of cultures and peoples. However, foreign invaders had raided and looted its riches for centuries. Mohammad Bin Qasim was the first to arrive from the Arab countries, under the Umayyad Caliphate at the turn of the 8th century. Upon returning to his land, he told others about the treasures that lay across South Asia and encouraged them to invade the land again. He had also noted there was not much of a fighting force to oppose them, so it would be easy for them to continue raiding the land. Jewels, pearls, gold, and other riches lay in abundance in temples across South Asia.

News travelled fast, and soon enough, many others followed in his footsteps to raid and plunder South Asia. The likes of Mahmud Ghazni (971-1030); Muhammad Ghori (1149-1206); Amir Timur (1336-1405); Nadir Shah (1688-1747); and Ahmad Shah Abdali (1722-1772) invaded and looted vast regions of South Asia. Temples were destroyed, people were slaughtered like helpless sheep, and women were kidnapped to be sold like animals in Kabul and other parts of the Arab world. This continued for almost a thousand years until the mighty Khalsa of Guru Gobind Singh not only offered stern opposition to the invaders but chased them all the way back into modern-day Afghanistan.

During the time of Sada Kaur, Ahmad Shah Durrani's grandson, Zaman Shah, was the King of Kabul. In 1797, he too felt the desire to follow in the footsteps of his forefathers and decided to launch an invasion via Panjab. He wanted to establish his rule, if not over all of South Asia, then certainly across the northern regions. He left with a small army, arrived in Lahore, and was able to take over with little resistance from the Bhangis, who dispersed into *Dharamsalas*. Zaman Shah remained in Lahore for a few months before deciding to head back to Kabul, only to return to Lahore in 1798.

An eighteen-year-old Ranjit Singh heard of what happened and was eager to launch an attack on Lahore. Overflowing with youthful exuberance, he decided this would be an opportune moment to announce his arrival as a major political player by sending a message to other rulers in the region. Within a few days, he dispatched a horseman to Sada Kaur in Batala with an invitation to join him in this endeavour.

Sada Kaur agreed with Ranjit Singh on the need to remove foreign invaders from their land. As a daughter of Guru Gobind Singh, she wanted to defend the country from ego-fuelled kings like Zaman Shah. At that time, Sada Kaur's fighting force numbered approximately ten thousand. She asked Rami to bring Dal Singh, Kamanda Singh, and Varyam Singh. Sada Kaur explained the situation to her leading generals and asked them for their input.

"In my view, Sarkar, we have the fighting force, and together with the Sukerchakia Misl, this would be a sure victory," stated Dal Singh.

"I agree, Sarkar, we have the advantage of striking when they least expect it. Zaman Shah has been entering Lahore at his leisure. Intoxicated by his own ego, he has taken over Lahore with the intention of once again invading Panjab, but his empire will soon crumble around him," added Kamanda Singh.

Varyam Singh echoed the views of his senior officers, stating, "Sarkar, when you marched on Sansar Chand, many people joined you en-route. You accepted the plea from my beloved Desa and liberated me from the fort of Pathankot, for which I am eternally grateful. I am ready to accept your command; just give us the order."

Listening to her trustworthy generals, Sada Kaur was pleased with their positive responses. These were exactly the answers she wanted to hear. She asked Rami to inform Ranjit Singh's horseman that the Kanaiya Misl would march with him to Lahore.

Sada Kaur took a seat, but as the three generals turned to walk out of the room, Rami came running back in.

"Sarkar, another messenger has just arrived from Gujranwala. He says Sardar Ranjit Singh left for Lahore as soon as he dispatched the first messenger."

Signalling her generals to sit back down, Sada Kaur stood up and roared, "Bring him to me instantly!"

A few moments later, Rami reappeared with the messenger, who explained that Ranjit Singh had left for Lahore with a small contingent to scope out Zaman Shah's troops on the ground. Sada Kaur knew Ranjit Singh was not capable of merely scoping out Zaman Shah; *his exuberance will get the better of him,* she thought.

"Sarkar, should we ready the troops and leave today?" asked Dal Singh.

"No, let us see how the young gun fairs in his mission. We shall await further instructions from the Sukerchakia head," said Sada Kaur.

As this conversation played out in Batala, Ranjit Singh had reached Lahore. Stationing his soldiers around the fort, he took up a vantage point and fired his guns into the air. When there was no reply from within the city walls, Ranjit Singh announced, "Oh, Zaman Shah, you are the grandson of Durrani, come outside the fort, the grandson of Charat Singh challenges you! You are sat inside the fort like a hyena; come outside and face this lion! My grandfather marked the end of Abdali, and I will remove you with my bare hands!"

Zaman Shah heard the gunfire outside the city walls and was informed of Ranjit Singh's word, but he did not move. He had heard great things about Ranjit Singh and Sada Kaur, and he knew the true power of the force that stood outside the fort. He also knew how Ranjit Singh's forefathers had beaten and humiliated his own ancestors. Peering out of the fort to catch a glimpse of the army of Sikhs that stood outside, Zaman Shah was unable to conjure the strength needed for words to respond to Ranjit Singh.

After a few hours of this stand-off, Ranjit Singh withdrew his forces and rode back to Gujranwala. Zaman Shah decided against his initial plans to march beyond the fort of Lahore and into Sikh territory. He gathered his army and announced that they would be returning to their country immediately.

During that time, there was a Muslim Nawab called Nazam Din Kasooria. He too had plans to rule over all of Panjab. Seeing the opportunity that had presented itself, he decided to take occupation of the fort of Lahore. News of this proposed move soon reached local leaders. Individuals like Ashak Muhammad, Mufti Muhammad Mukaram, and Hakim Hakam Rai travelled to Gujranwala to inform Ranjit Singh of his plans.

They were concerned for the welfare of the people of Lahore and did not want Nawab Nazam Din Kasooria to take over Lahore. Arriving in Gujranwala, they pleaded with Ranjit Singh to bring his army back to Lahore, where the locals would greet them with open arms.

Smiling, Ranjit Singh assured them of his protection and immediately left for Batala to see Sada Kaur. En-route, Ranjit Singh felt a sense of good fortune; he knew in his heart this was the beginning of something special. As he rode east towards Batala, crossing the River Ravi, all the illustrious accounts from Sikh history were replayed in his mind.

# 15.

It was the early months of autumn, and Rami was assisting Kamanda Singh in the stables. She always looked forward to spending time with her horse and thoroughly enjoyed helping Kamanda Singh with routine cleaning and maintenance chores around the stables. As Rami washed down her horse gently, she looked towards Kamanda Singh and caught her husband lovingly smiling back.

"You look beautiful today, dear," commented Kamanda Singh, as he flung some saddles over his shoulder and walked over to his cleaning table.

Rami smiled. She was now thirty years old and had been married to Kamanda Singh for seven years. It had been fourteen years since the day she had run through the streets of Batala with news of Gurbaksh Singh's death. Over the years, Rami had become Sada Kaur's most trusted aide, both in administrative affairs and in battle. She rode alongside Dal Singh at the front of the army whenever the Kanaiya Misl had ventured out of Batala to launch an attack.

Kamanda Singh was a powerful man, tall and strong, but he was a gentle giant. His love for horses and seeing to their every need, before and during battle, was his top priority. As a skilled swordsman too, he had recently taken over as deputy to Dal Singh and assisted Sultan Singh, the ironsmith. There was great camaraderie amongst the top commanders and fighters of Sada Kaur's Kanaiya Misl, and she often encouraged competitive battles and sports between her army personnel.

Rami and Kamanda had two twin children, Rattan Singh and Sobha Singh, aged five. They, too, spent their days playing amongst the stables under the watchful guise of their parents. Rami herself was an orphan child with no siblings. Sada Kaur had taken her in off the streets when she was just ten years old. Through her loyalty and friendship, Rami was now like family; her children would often sit in the garden with Sada Kaur whom they lovingly referred to as 'Massi ji'.

"Sardar Ranjit Singh is here! Sardar Ranjit Singh is here!" shouted Rattan, as he came running into the stables.

Hearing the sound of hooves in the courtyard behind her, Rami stood up and peered through the stable doors. She noticed Ranjit Singh had ridden in, unannounced, with a few horsemen of the Sukerchakia Misl, which he now led. Since his marriage to Mehtab Kaur, Sada Kaur had handed full responsibility of the Misl back to Sukerchakia, although she had remained an important advisor. Sensing he had important news, Rami placed the wet towel to one side and informed Kamanda Singh she would be back shortly.

As Ranjit Singh entered the gates, Rami hurriedly ran across the courtyard into the palace. She turned up the staircase, along the hallway, and entered Sada Kaur's room. The queen was resting, as she had come down with a high temperature the night before.

"Excuse me, Sarkar, but Sardar Ranjit Singh has just arrived," said Rami.

Turning over to look at Rami, Sada Kaur smiled and slowly lifted herself from the bed. She ventured over to the window that overlooked the courtyard.

"Ah, my son has arrived! Rami, please seat them in the *divan khana*. I shall be down shortly."

Rami nodded and swiftly headed back down the hallway. As she skipped down the stairs, Rami called for Taro and Basanti to ready breakfast and refreshments for their guests. Upon reaching the *divan khana,* she arranged the chairs and then headed over to greet Ranjit Singh and his guards.

"Vaheguru ji ka Khalsa Vaheguru ji ki Fateh," said Rami, clasping her palms together, "this is a pleasant surprise."

Smiling, Ranjit Singh returned the greeting with equal fervour. Turning to the stables, he said, "Sister, please also ask Kamanda Singh and Dal Singh to join us this morning. I have some very important news."

*That is an unusual request; he's never asked for them by name before,* thought Rami, before motioning for Ranjit Singh to enter the palace. Rami then gathered Kamanda Singh and Dal Singh and headed towards the *divan khana,* where Sada Kaur sat waiting with Ranjit Singh.

Rami stood and listened as Ranjit Singh informed Sada Kaur of what happened in Lahore, and the subsequent request from the residents. After listening to Ranjit Singh explain the whole situation, Sada Kaur spoke, "I have been thinking for some time now about ways to unite and bring Lahore under the sovereign flags of the Khalsa. We have already established rule over Hoshiarpur and Kangra, all the way to Jammu, but without taking Lahore, we cannot name you King of all Panjab. I am aware the Bhangi and Ramgharia Misls stand in our way, and it would seem this Nawab Kasooria, too, is one we will need to deal with swiftly. I have enough soldiers in our armies to not only mount an attack on Lahore but also take it!"

"There will not be much of a fight in Lahore, Mother. We do not need to take many soldiers. The Bhangis will no doubt be intoxicated and will offer little opposition. I think we will need no more than seven to eight hundred troops on the ground," said Ranjit Singh.

"No, son. When one goes hunting for deer, it is wise to prepare for an encounter with lions. We should not take any fewer than seven to eight thousand horses. It would be naïve of us to assume they will just roll over; it is better to prepare for a larger battle than to return empty-handed," replied Sada Kaur.

"I will take Lahore in one day; then we shall march on Kasur, Multan, Attock, Peshawar, and Kashmir and spread Sikh rule across the land. If I have your support, Mother, anything is possible." Ranjit Singh was overcome with excitement at the prospect of establishing a new and expansive Raj.

Sada Kaur nodded and said, "Yes, I will also do everything in my power to secure Sikh rule over distant lands too. What I want is for the Rajputs, Marathas, and the British to recognise our sovereignty too."

Ranjit Singh stood up and asked Sada Kaur to make immediate plans to begin her journey and meet him with her forces at the Shalamar Bagh, situated some five kilometres outside Lahore. Sada Kaur agreed and headed out of the room. Ranjit Singh rode back to Gujranwala to ready his army.

Sada Kaur walked down the grand corridor of her palace and took the flight of stairs to the first floor. She headed towards the room where Guru Granth Sahib was placed on a raised platform, studded in jewels and covered with fine cloth. Before beginning any task, a Sikh always seeks the Guru's blessings by taking a *Hukamnama,* reciting *Gurbani,* and offering an *Ardas.* Sada Kaur had always done this, and she had utmost faith and confidence in this important Sikh protocol.

Upon taking a *Hukamnama,* Sada Kaur sat in meditation for a while. She allowed her mind to become still and focus on the greatness of the Guru's Word. She had been in this place many times before. With great clarity of thought and concentration on *Akal Purakh,* Sada Kaur stood up with folded hands and began her *Ardas.* In this *Ardas,* she announced her plans to launch an attack on Lahore and asked for the support and protection of Vaheguru in her mission to establish Sikh rule over all of Panjab.

Those brave warriors who take to the battlefield always have faith in two things. One is full faith in Vaheguru, and the other is full faith in their weapons. Before completing her *Ardas,* Sada Kaur also recited many Dasam Bani passages in praise of weapons and righteous warfare. Evoking the spirit of *Shaheeds,* the countless Sikh martyrs that came before her, she bowed in reverence and gracefully walked out of the room.

Sada Kaur turned to Dal Singh and said, "*Fauja tyar karo,* ready the army."

"Sarkar, are we taking the whole *fauj*?"

"No, only half. The other half will remain here to stand guard over Batala."

"Yes, Sarkar."

"The moment we have been working towards has finally arrived. We have won many battles and regained control over various territories, bringing peace and prosperity to vast regions of Panjab; however, we now stand on the brink of taking Lahore and solidifying Sikh Raj to an even greater extent."

Rami listened attentively as Sada Kaur continued, "Let us not falter in this stand; with the blessings of *Akal Purakh* and the support of Sikh martyrs who continue to guide and inspire us, we shall remove the tyrants from Lahore and hoist the sovereign flags of the Khalsa Panth all over Panjab."

Turning to Rami and Kamanda Singh, Sada Kaur said, "Please ready Vayu and assist Dal Singh in preparing the fauj. We will take two cannons with us. Inform Ram Singh, Sham Singh, and Gopal Singh that they are to take care of matters in my absence."

Dal Singh and Kamanda Singh nodded, called a *Fateh,* and left to ready the army. Rami accompanied Sada Kaur to her room. Knowing her health was not a hundred percent, Rami then asked some of the other servants to prepare a strong concoction of ground herbs to help Sada Kaur prepare for the march on Lahore. Rami watched as her queen prepared herself for the march, lovingly tying her crown, interlaced with chainmail, before placing a select assortment of small sharp weapons around it. Sada Kaur then tightened a *kamarkasa* around her waist where she added further hand-held weapons such as a *katar, peshkabz,* and *kukri*. On that day, she wore two swords, placed a rifle over her shoulders, and, resting her hands on the hilt of her swords, Sada Kaur spoke, "Rami, today is an auspicious day. Today we get to show the whole world how daughters of Guru Gobind Singh fight. May the spirit of Mai Bhago, Bibi Sharan Kaur, and countless other mothers and sisters of this glorious Panth guide us and lead us to victory. Akal Sahai!"

With that, Sada Kaur took the glass of mixed herbs and hot water, knocked it back, and headed for the courtyard, where her trustworthy Vayu stood waiting to lead her to Lahore. The *Ranjit Nagara* could be heard from within the palace walls. The sound of horses' hooves soon followed as a contingent of approximately five thousand warriors of the Kanaiya Misl left for Lahore with the fearless Sada Kaur leading from the front.

# 16.

Lahore is famous for its Anarkali Bazaar. To the west of this market, there are large gardens. Before 1799, the gardens were named after Wazir Khan; they were open and had a variety of flowers and large trees. The combined Sikh forces of Kanaiya and Sukerchakia Misls assembled in these gardens. Many of the older residents of Lahore had experienced the days of Abdali's invasions, so out of fear, had remained indoors. Bhangi Misl leaders such as Gujjar Singh and Sahib Singh locked the main gates of the city. They took refuge within the city's inner walls, like mice scampering to hide from the swooping claws of the falcon.

"I will head towards the Delhi gate and station our soldiers, while you make your way to Lohari Shah Aalmi Gate and do the same there. Bring no harm to women or children, and do not strike an unarmed man. Do not loot or plunder the locals' homes or shops. Uphold the Khalsa battle stratagem."

Sada Kaur gave Ranjit Singh this instruction and then turned to head towards the Delhi gate. She was at the front of her *fauj*. With Rami on one side and Dal Singh on the other, Sada Kaur moved forward with her unsheathed sword raised high in her right hand. With Vaheguru on her lips and war on her mind, Sada Kaur was fully armed for a bloody battle. She knew in her heart this moment would define her reign as head of the Kanaiya Misl and pave the way for a new political reality in Panjab.

As Sada Kaur neared the Delhi gate, she noticed the Bhangis sitting outside. She let out a fierce battle cry and ordered her soldiers to attack. As they entered the city walls, Nawab Kasooria's men were caught entirely off-guard. The first blow came from Sada Kaur's mighty sword. She took on the form of a warrior goddess in the battlefield, removing the heads of those who stood in front of her in one sweeping stroke. Seeing their leader fight with such ferocity and power, the Sikhs of the Kanaiya Misl let out loud battle cries and charged forward with even more force.

"Crush the enemies!"

"Bole So Nihaal, Sat Sri Akal!"

"Lahore will be the new Sikh capital!"

Shouting such words of encouragement, Sada Kaur's Kanaiya Misl sliced through the enemy with ease, each one taking out eight to ten enemy combatants. Dal Singh was a man possessed, tearing through the ego-fuelled soldiers who stood in his way. His swords moved with such speed and ferocity it was hard to make out which strike hit which body as his hands propelled through the air.

Just behind Dal Singh, Rami and Kamanda Singh were dancing on the battlefield, simultaneously annihilating those who came forward to strike them. Desa, too, was not far behind, moving through Nawab Kasooria's mercenaries like a silent assassin. Her close arm combat was extraordinary, one of the reasons Sada Kaur had picked her to fight with her unit at the front. As her *katar* plunged through one body, she violently twisted her wrist before ripping the enemy to shreds.

A further contingent of troops was sent out by Kasooria. He himself joined a small band of three others. The four horsemen, cladded in green and white uniforms, charged towards Sada Kaur, who stood like a mountain in the middle of the Lahore battlefield.

As the horses charged, Sada Kaur began her *pentra.* She moved her feet, stepping in and then out, turning her body at an angle to complement her stride. With each step, she edged forward towards the charging enemy, her gaze never leaving her target. In full flow, with the horses closing in, Sada Kaur crossed her arms down to her waist before revealing two *peshkabz* tucked in her *kamarkasa.* The blades glistened in the air as she raised them, drawing a cross in the air in front of her face, before leaning back with full force as she launched the blades, which whistled through the air, striking the first two horsemen straight in the forehead. The riders collapsed sideways into a heap in the middle, causing the front two horses to split just metres away from Sada Kaur. As they did, this revealed the two other horsemen. As Sada Kaur's hands came down from the momentum of having just thrown the two *peshkabz,* they landed on the hilts of her two swords. In a magnificent fit of rage, Sada Kaur unsheathed both swords. Swinging them over her head, she charged towards the advancing horses. Upon seeing this, Kasooria halted and turned off to the side, leaving his soldier to face the full force of Sada Kaur's swords.

Turning around, the coward's eyes witnessed Sada Kaur leap up into the air, with swords out like the wings of a swooping blue hawk. In the blink of an eye, Sada Kaur landed on the ground as his comrade's headless body rode off into the distance.

"Hai Allah, this woman is the form of *AL-Lat*!"

As Kasooria turned around, he was met by the striking blow of Rami's arrow, which ripped through his torso, instantly bringing him to the ground.

As they neared the gates of the fort, turning to her troops, Sada Kaur shouted, "Ready the cannons!"

Just as she had made the order to prepare the cannons, a set of guards standing on the outer periphery of the fort surrendered. They felt it was their only option upon witnessing the fighting prowess of the Sikhs that stood before them. As family men, they thought, *it is better we save ourselves and welcome our new leader with open arms. After all, these are not Durranis, Mughals, or the British. They are one of our own. Everyone knows of their bravery and generous rule.*

The guards threw their weapons to the ground, knelt down, and happily accompanied the Sikh entourage. Without attacking any of the homes or shops, Sada Kaur led her warriors through the streets towards the fort. From the other side, Ranjit Singh and the Sukerchakia fighters came galloping forward. The Sikhs now surrounded the fort of Lahore. The residents of Lahore, who had previously remained indoors, upon seeing that no innocent person was harmed, and nor was there any looting or plundering, stepped outside. The local leaders who had travelled to Gujranwala and pleaded with Ranjit Singh to save and protect them presented themselves before Sada Kaur.

"The owner of this fort is Chet Singh, and he is currently sitting inside the fort. All the entrances are closed," explained Ranjit Singh.

"I see; well then ..." started Sada Kaur.

Ranjit Singh interrupted, "Bring forward the cannons. If the doors of this fort remain closed, we shall bring it all down."

"No, son. There is no need to destroy such a well-built fortress with walls as big as mountains. We shall wait. We have taken the city; Chet Singh cannot remain in the fort for long. Send a message asking him to vacate the fort. We shall allow him to leave with his family. Wherever he wishes to go, he can go," came the wise words of Sada Kaur.

Ranjit Singh accepted this order and sent the message with one of his horsemen. Inside the fort, Chet Singh hadn't come outside for fear of being killed. However, upon reading the letter, he was instantly relieved and accepted the conditions. He gathered his belongings and his entourage and quickly left the fort.

This was the fort built by the Mughals. Many powers, including the Mughals, Pathans, Durranis, and Iranians, had occupied the fort and brought misery to the peoples of Panjab. It was opposite this same fort that the fifth light of Guru Nanak, Guru Arjan Dev ji, had been martyred on 30th May, 1606. The Mughals and Pathans once thought that no one else would have the strength or power to ever take it from them.

On 25th April 1799, Sada Kaur and her trusted band of warriors, comprised of Rami, Desa, Kamada Singh, and Dal Singh, led Ranjit Singh, along with thousands of brave and fearless Sikh warriors from both the Kanaiya and Sukerchakia Misl, into the fort. As they entered the inner sanctum of the fort, Sada Kaur meditated on *Akal Purakh* and whispered, *"Dhan Kalgiawale, Shah-i-Shehanshah, Sahib Sri Guru Gobind Singh ji Maharaj."*

# 17.

Following the victory over Lahore, Ranjit Singh was crowned as the Maharaja of all Panjab. He exercised an absolute and arbitrary sway over the people, becoming chief judge and referee in all questions of governance. While Ranjit Singh absorbed the limelight, Rani Sada Kaur committed herself to strengthening the Raj. In the first twenty years of the Sikh Empire, she was instrumental in waging wars to expand Sikh territory, alongside legendary warriors such as Hari Singh Nalwa, Akali Phula Singh, and Sham Singh Attarivala.

Haripur-Hazara is a mountainous region to the north of Peshawar. The peaks of Malika and Gagan are two famous mountains that stand within this beautiful region. There are many different freshwater streams and waterfalls, lush green trees, and wild plants that grow many different flowers and fruits. Gandhgir is another very famous mountain in the region of Haripur-Hazara.

It was the month of December 1818. The mountains of Hazara and Kashmir were covered in snow. In the foothills of the Gandhgir, under the entrance to a small cave, Sada Kaur was standing looking over the lower regions that lay before her. Beside the cave, there was a large rock, where Sada Kaur had positioned her horse. In her right hand, Sada Kaur held a sword drenched in the blood of her enemies. This was the same sword that she had kissed as she vowed to make Panjab a formidable country, following the martyrdom of her husband, thirty-three years ago. The sword had been her constant companion for over three decades.

Sada Kaur was no longer a young woman; she was now fifty-six years old. The hair on her head had started to turn white. Although she was a lot older, there had been no change in her spirit, bravery, strength, or the sparkle in her eyes that had led Sikh Rule from one victory to the next. Her big, round eyes were scanning the ground for enemy combatants.

Despite leading Ranjit Singh to establish a formidable army and expansive rule, Sada Kaur's sword was still swinging in all its glory to defend and further Sikh Raj. This was the Raj in which Sada Kaur had made Ranjit Singh the ruler of Lahore, Maharaja of all of Panjab, where coins were struck in the name of Guru Nanak Dev ji, and sovereign flags of the Khalsa flew over Kasur, Multan, *Amrit*sar, Jammu, and Kashmir.

Even the high peaks of Hazara were in awe of the courageous soul who was prowling its rough terrain - the warrior queen who had spent thirty years leading and winning battles for Ranjit Singh and the Sikh Empire. In her early days, Vayu had been a loyal horse, but at that moment, Gaggar, another brave horse, was her trustworthy steed. The duty to uphold *dharam*, protect the weak, oppose the oppressor and advance *Khalsa Raj* was why Sada Kaur that day was chasing the thieving Pathans. She had spent the whole day in battle and didn't tire once. Leading from the front, she continued to inspire other fighters to defeat some of the region's most feared Pathans.

Sada Kaur was also very happy that day because her grandson, Sher Singh, was fighting with her. Sher Singh was like her in many ways, both brave and strong. Just like Sada Kaur had raised his father, Ranjit Singh, and trained him well, she had also spent many years training and preparing Sher Singh to be an excellent swordsman and rider.

The Khalsa Army was spread far and wide from the cave's opening where Sada Kaur stood. The whole ground before them was soaked with Pathans' blood whose bodies were scattered across the battlefield. Some had been cut in half, others had missing legs or arms. The locals were overcome with relief and joy when they heard the Khalsa Army had arrived to save them from the Pathans, who were constantly harassing them.

Sada Kaur climbed on to the rock where Gaggar stood. The image of her husband, whom she had never forgotten, encircled her mind. She felt he was close by, always watching and protecting her in spirit form. She heard him say, *"Sada Kaur, I congratulate you! You are a great warrior who has led the Khalsa to the greatest of heights. With your bravery, you have not only beaten enemies on the battleground, but you've also beaten the internal enemies of lust, anger, attachment, greed, and ego. You have stayed loyal to me your whole life. You are the embodiment of a true wife; your love, faith, and bravery are eternal."*

*This is all by the Grace and Will of Akal Purakh Vaheguru,* spoke Sada Kaur's inner voice.

Sada Kaur had climbed upon the large rock to scope out any remaining Pathans who may have been hiding in front of her. She had already won the first day's battle. The Pathans with whom she had been fighting were no ordinary Pathans but were considered some of the most feared, stone-hearted, and battle-hardened Pathans of the region. They were those who considered Panjab and the rest of South Asia their hunting ground. In the past, whenever they felt like venturing towards Panjab to loot and plunder, they had so done freely. However, this encounter had awoken them to a new reality.

Gaggar, the horse that Sada Kaur was riding in battle, was a tall Arabian horse. Its large, powerful hooves had broken some of the rocks on the ground as it galloped through the battlefield. During the battle, Sada Kaur had used her large spear, her rifle, and her sword. Upon seeing her move through the battle, the Pathans were struck with both awe and fear; wherever she encountered a Pathan, she would leave him in pieces on the ground. Many of the Pathans had conspired to kill her, but with the help of Desa, Sada Kaur had remained out of their reach.

When the Pathans saw no victory in sight, they started to run away from the battle. The Khalsa Army had caught many of them, stripped them of their weapons, and eventually secured victory. As Sada Kaur stood on the large rock, one of the officers came over and said, "Mata ji, I'm afraid I have bad news. Some of the enemies have killed our brave Ram Dyal and his contingent."

"How did that happen?" asked Sada Kaur.

"In his naivety, young Ram Dyal chased the Pathans so far out of the battlefield that he ended up in a village, where many other Pathans surrounded and killed them."

Sada Kaur looked towards the direction in which the officer was pointing as he relayed the story.

"I want you to bring Sham Singh and the other Sardars to me immediately. We are going to find the rest of these Pathans, even if we have to move these mountains!" roared Sada Kaur.

Sardar Sham Singh Attari was a well-respected and loyal member of the Khalsa Army. Sher Singh was a young but brave warrior, and Hukma Singh, another Sardar, did not fear anyone. All three presented themselves before Sada Kaur. She had climbed off the rock and was now mounted on Gaggar. Addressing the three chiefs, Sada Kaur said, "The enemy has taken the young life of brave Ram Dyal. Your Maharaja loved Ram Dyal like his own son. What will you say to your king? What news will you take back to Mohkam Chand (Ram Dyal's grandfather) and Divan Moti Ram (Ram Dyal's father)? From me, your order is to find every single Pathan that remains and send him to the next world! We will need to wait until the night passes, but come early morning, we shall launch another attack. Turn over every large and small rock and look in every cave – I want you to provide a befitting response to his martyrdom!"

All of the Sardars listened and accepted the order from their commander-in-chief. Early next morning, the Khalsa Army sought out the Pathans; many more were killed, and others ran away. One particular group of Pathans threw down their weapons and pleaded mercy, asking to join the services of the Khalsa. Sardar Sham Singh took them to Sada Kaur.

"The Khalsa is not interested in looting or enslaving anyone. Our job is to fight oppression and protect the weak. In a state of ego and spiritual darkness, you have brought much misery and death to your own neighbours. The Khalsa had to march here and deliver justice. Hindus, Muslims, and Sikhs are all from that Vaheguru; we are all one. This is the teaching of Guru Nanak Dev ji. Everyone should live together in peace. Khalsa rule shall not interfere with your own choice of faith or practice. If you can accept this, then you shall all be freed."

The Pathans were humbled by the show of compassion from one of the Khalsa Army's fiercest generals. They listened and accepted every single word that Sada Kaur spoke. Vowing never to harass the innocent and weak, the Pathans were set free.

In this way, Sada Kaur led the Sardars to other victories through other small villages in the Hazara region, right the way up to Kashmir. Having expanded *Khalsa Raj* with the sword, a victorious Sada Kaur headed back to Lahore. She entered Maharaja Ranjit Singh's Darbar, bowed, and handed awards and honours from the king to her brave Khalsa Army. Many had heard of Sada Kaur's victory over the northern territories. *Bhatts* and *Kavishris* soon assembled and sang war ballads in praise of her bravery.

# 18.

Sada Kaur had raised Ranjit Singh like her own child since the early 1790s. Even though she had suffered great personal loss in her youth, Sada Kaur had shown great wisdom and foresight. She had been widowed at the age of twenty-two, and that too by the actions of Ranjit Singh's father, Maha Singh, but Sada Kaur was a resilient woman. She had full faith in the Guru and *Akal Purakh*, and the will to follow Guru Gobind Singh's command to establish political rule for the Khalsa. To not only forgive those who took her husband, but to accept their dying wish and save their Misl, protect their son, and then wage wars to make him supreme ruler of all Panjab; it takes a special woman to do that.

Sada Kaur endured personal loss, sleepless nights, and battle wounds but placed Ranjit Singh over her own ambitions to rule. In her mind, she always wanted to establish a kingdom that worked on the Guru-inspired Sikh principle of *Sarbat Da Bhalla*; welfare for all. If she had wanted, Sada Kaur could have established a large and prosperous territory of her own - with a strong and resourceful army, she would have been one of the most formidable forces in Panjab. But Sada Kaur wanted to break away from the pitfalls of small, individual territories and did everything in her power to ensure her son-in-law, whom she treated as her very own, was in the best position to unite all of Panjab. This had been Sada Kaur's mission ever since she had first heard of the inter-Misl quarrels back in 1778.

A few more years had passed since those victories in Kashmir. The year was 1823, and Sada Kaur was now sixty-one. The whole world knew of Maharaja Ranjit Singh. The Lahore Darbar included an array of experienced and ambitious ministers who had developed vast amounts of influence over Ranjit Singh. The *Darbar* would often receive gifts from monarchs in Nepal, Kabul, Russia, France, and England, as a show of respect and friendship.

Various *divans* were held in the forts where many great poets like Hasham would come and sing the praises of Ranjit Singh and the Lahore Darbar. The Maharaja had married ten times; the treasury was overflowing with dazzling jewels and diamonds, including the Kohinoor; admirers of the king brought daily offerings; the death penalty had been abolished; education was available to all; the arts were flourishing, and the economy of Panjab was very strong. The Maharaja treated everyone equally, and in return, they were loyal subjects of the crown.

The Khalsa Army was one of the most powerful and feared armies in all of South Asia. Soldiers from Italy, France, and England had travelled to join Ranjit Singh's army, and he had placed some of them in charge of large units. There were many factories where guns, cannons, swords, and different types of weapons were made for the Khalsa Army. The Sikhs were stationed in barracks across all of Panjab, along the Himalayas, and all the way up to the Khyber Pass. Maharaja Ranjit Singh's Raj's establishment was possible only because of Sada Kaur's faith in Guru and her long-term vision.

One day, while sitting in his *mahal,* Ranjit Singh called for Sada Kaur. When the veteran warrior arrived, Ranjit Singh said, "Have you heard? Rani Daya Kaur of Ambala has passed away."

"No, I hadn't heard that."

"Yes, she has passed away. The British have taken over her territory with ease because she had no son."

"That is very sad news."

"You have been blessed by Vaheguru with many things; there isn't much that you do not have. You have two grandsons. But from a legal standpoint, having no son must be a concern for you."

"A concern?"

"Yes. A concern because you are the owner of Forts Vadni, Himmatpur, and ruler of the surrounding 15 localities. I wish to send the Khalsa Army and take ownership of these while you are still alive. Otherwise, it leaves you vulnerable to an attack and siege from the British. You've already handed some localities to Sher Singh."

If anyone other than Ranjit Singh had spoken this way to her, Sada Kaur would've taken his head off. She was completely shocked by what she heard. She never thought Ranjit Singh of all people, whom she had raised herself, could ever say such words; it was as if he had just plunged a dagger into her heart.

The brave and courageous warrior queen who had never refrained from battle, who had overcome the greatest of foes, was suddenly overcome with a sense of deep distress and anxiety. Those words, *from a legal standpoint, having no son must be a concern for you,* began to play over and over in her head. Her body felt weak, and for the first time, she felt alone. A voice inside her head now said, *I don't have a son, I don't have a son.*

Sada Kaur momentarily lost all sense of where she was. She forgot about her daughter and her grandsons. She thought of Gurbaksh Singh, who had been a constant source of strength and stability for her, but at that moment, she could not quieten that inner voice. For the first time in her life, Sada Kaur felt the void of having no son born of her womb. The man who stood in front of her appeared foreign. He was not the Ranjit Singh she had spent her younger years raising and nurturing with love and joy. He had become a stranger since he'd found a new circle of advisers comprised of the Dogra brothers. She thought to herself, *if I had a son of my own, I would never have had to hear such words.*

Overcome with grief, Sada Kaur's eyes became tearful. The heart that had never known any fear was suddenly overcome with a feeling of deep sorrow. Sada Kaur managed to keep the tears from falling. She mustered some courage and softly said, "We should not hurry this; let us think it over."

"Why?" asked Ranjit Singh.

"At the moment, there are cordial relations between the Lahore Darbar and the *firanghis.* Also, I've noticed since you've taken on these new Dogra advisors, you seem to have acted on impulse and made many rash decisions in matters concerning the Raj."

"Nonsense! This is just a doubt of yours. My advisors only seek the best for me and the Lahore Darbar. Times are changing again, Mother, it is important we secure our position and do not fall prey to our adversaries."

"Son, I raised you with my own hands. I know you, and I know this is not your decision. All I ask at this time is that we refrain from acting in haste. Let us think about it more and discuss the matter further."

"We need to act promptly. Delaying matters will only serve the interests of the *firanghi;* the British."

"Whether it serves their interests or not, I know it certainly serves the interests of the Dogras who have been trying to cause a rift between you and me for some time now."

"That is not true, just the doubts of your own mind."

"No. Not my doubts, son; this is reality."

"Whatever! We can discuss those matters later. Tell me, should we send the Khalsa Army to take over the Fort of Vadni? I need an answer from you today."

"I am heading to Batala today. I will think and let you know. Let's not rush this. There are other pressing matters."

"So, you will not give me an answer today?"

"No. I am leaving now. I don't feel well; my head is spinning."

"Should I call the doctor?"

"No, there is no need for that."

Saying this, Sada Kaur stood up and quickly walked out of the *mahal*. Ranjit Singh watched her but was unable to say anything more.

# 19.

Sada Kaur was walking in the gardens of her *haveli* in Batala, dressed in all white. Her face was now expressionless and riddled with lines of old age. As she walked around the gardens, she was in deep thought, still reeling from that fateful conversation in the *mahal* of Maharaja Ranjit Singh.

Many of her old companions had left her. Like Vayu, Gaggar had fallen in battle. In their place stood new Arabian horses. Loyal aides like Rami and Desa, too, had perished over time. The brave and trustworthy Dal Singh, who once stood beside her like an immovable mountain, also had passed away. There were new faces everywhere. No matter which direction Sada Kaur looked towards, everything in the familiar setting of her own *haveli* appeared foreign. This added to her deepened state of anxiety, which hadn't left her since the conversation with Ranjit Singh.

As she walked over to the mango tree, Sada Kaur reached up and plucked out a ripe fruit. She turned it around in her hand and said to herself, "Just like my husband, you too have become a distant memory."

Looking at the mango tree, she said, "The passage of time will one day uproot you too. These gardens, the well, and those beautiful flowers will one day grow weary, face neglect, and become a sight for sore eyes."

Sada Kaur wandered over to the well and looked inside. In the pure water, she saw her reflection. While she had maintained her sharp features, signs of old age were visible across her face and neck. She had just begun to notice the wrinkles when her grandson, Sher Singh, came running over. He was a fine and handsome seventeen-year-old, full of life and vibrance, with a budding moustache and short beard.

Sada Kaur immediately knew something was wrong. Normally Sher Singh would come to her smiling and laughing, but today his young face was full of rage and anger.

Just before he reached her, Sher Singh shouted, "Mata ji, Mata ji!"

*"Hanji, Shere, ki hoya?"* Yes Sher, what is the matter?

"I have some very bad news!"

"What bad news, son?"

“I have come to seek your permission to launch a revolt against my father, the Maharaja!”

“What?!” Sada Kaur shouted back.

“You wish to raise a revolt against your own father, but why? What has happened, son?”

“A great big betrayal; he is making a huge mistake.”

“Betrayal? Mistake? With you, son?”

“With you, Mata ji, with you.”

“Me? How can he betray me? Son, what you're saying doesn't make sense. Please, tell me the whole matter properly. What has happened?”

Sada Kaur took Sher Singh into her arms and embraced him tightly. She looked at him and said, “Tell me openly. What has my Ranjit Singh, an honest and fair man, done that you are accusing him of betraying me? What could possibly make you want to raise a revolt against the king? Against your own father?”

“What can I say, Mata ji, I don't know what to think; my mind is overcome with rage. My blood is boiling. He is about to carry out a great sin, completely against *dharam*. A deed unworthy of a Sikh.”

"Son, take a deep breath and tell me everything from the beginning. The Maharaja is your father. It is not nice to see his son speak in this manner. What has caused you to say these things?"

Hesitating slightly, Sher Singh looked up and said, "The Maharaja has today issued an order … an order which forbids you from any political involvement with the Lahore Darbar and restricts you from leading any military unit. The Maharaja has stated you can stay wherever you wish; Lahore, Batala, or *Amrit*sar, but you are to be stripped of all military and political positions with immediate effect."

Hesitating again, Sher Singh looked up and then said, "The order also reads you are to stay housebound and just recite Vaheguru Vaheguru."

"I see; is that his order? But why?" asked Sada Kaur.

"The order has been issued because you refused to give up the forts of Vadni and Himmatpur. The Maharaja hurriedly ordered Gulab Singh Dogra's military unit to move towards Vadni. On the other side, news of this broke within the *firanghi* camp, so they took this as an act of aggression and sent their troops. Now the British flags fly over Vadni Fort. The Khalsa Army under Gulab Singh Dogra was forced to retreat. The Maharaja was greatly angered by this. He was advised to imprison you, but he was unable to issue that order."

Sada Kaur listened as Sher Singh continued, "Tell me, Mata ji, what harm did you bring to him? You raised him from the age of ten, nurtured him with all your love and support. Is this what you deserve? What sort of man would do such a thing? Effectively imprison his own god-like mother? Is this not a betrayal? Is it not unrighteous? Well, I cannot sit around and allow him to do this!"

"*Shahzade!* Children can make mistakes and disown their parents, but a loving parent will never disown or wish any harm upon their child. Blinded by the attachment to political power and through his own ministers' deceitful actions, the Maharaja is making a mistake. But over time, he will realise this. The reality is, son, that I am old now. In fact, I wish to rest and spend my days in remembrance of *Akal Purakh* Vaheguru. I am prepared to accept this order. He is my son-in-law, after all. I have spent decades building the power and strength that he today commands. I will not defy him now, even if he decides to imprison me or even hang me! This is the Will of Vaheguru."

"Mata ji, I cannot allow this to happen. I have heard that Gulab Singh Dogra will be sent here tomorrow to issue the order."

"There's no need to worry, son. Please listen to me. Now go. You must go and get some rest."

Young Sher Singh accepted his Nani's instruction and walked out of the gardens towards his room. As he disappeared into the *haveli*, Sada Kaur let out a large sigh. She completely understood her grandson's anger and desire to raise a revolt. After all, the Maharaja was making a huge mistake. But Sada Kaur also knew deep down in her heart that this was not his order. It was the order of a confused and vulnerable man who had acted on impulse, despite her prior warning.

*Oh, dear. The danger that I feared has come true,* Sada Kaur began thinking. *Ranjit Singh should not have done this. Now is not the time to start a war with the firanghi; he is very powerful and has the backing of the monarch of England. Whereas there is no imminent danger while Ranjit Singh and I live, I know the firanghi is waiting for the day that we pass so that he can pounce upon our country and destroy what we have built.*

*While standing on the foothills of a large mountain, man forgets about the ground he once walked upon. He also forgets that at any point, he can slip off the mountain and land back on the ground, but in a state far worse than when he started.*

Sada Kaur continued to think of the grave mistake Ranjit Singh had made. She had never liked the Dogras from the moment they arrived in the Darbar. She knew they posed a great risk to Ranjit Singh and the very foundations of the Raj that she had cemented. However, Sada Kaur also knew that there was no option for her but to accept the order. If she accepted Sher Singh's request and supported him in a revolt, it would break Sikh Rule overnight. The British had already annexed the region of Malwa. She knew, in all her wisdom and foresight, that she had to accept and endure this order.

Sada Kaur decided to leave Batala and head for *Amrit*sar. She was content with this as it gave her the opportunity to live in the Guru's city and spend her final days in remembrance of *Akal Purakh* Vaheguru. This was her last wish; to secure a place at the sacred feet of the Guru.

On that day, the mighty Sada Kaur, who had spent her whole life offering wise and loving counsel to everyone she had encountered, had no one to turn to. She wandered into her room, gathered her belongings into one small bag, and prepared to leave for *Amrit*sar.

# 20.

The *firanghi* was a very cunning enemy. Everywhere he went, he not only conquered entire landmasses but also eliminated any memory of their glorious traditions and history. Entire cultures and languages were wiped out by the coloniser. This was done to prevent their newly-enslaved subjects from reading about their brave ancestors and realising their true worth and value. An enslaved mind makes for an obedient citizen. After invading Panjab and taking occupation in 1849, the colonisers did exactly this. Panjab was suppressed on all fronts. Doubts were cast upon Sikh history and tradition, attempts were made to distort the true meaning of *Gurbani,* and buildings of historical significance were destroyed and replaced with European-style architecture. Christian missionaries were given free rein to spread their gospel.

In 1874, in the north *parikarma* of Sri Darbar Sahib, a clock tower was erected, which has since been taken down. The clock tower was designed in classical European Gothic style as a show of power, authority, and control. It was originally supposed to be a church; however, that plan was side-lined. The clock tower was built where the *bungas* of

*Sardars* Sher Singh Attarivala and Ajit Singh Ladve once stood. The British had torn down those *bungas* because these two *Sardars* had offered unrelenting resistance to their occupation of Panjab.

It was amongst those *bungas* that Sada Kaur, too, had a small *bunga* where she lived following her move from Batala. During British colonial rule over Panjab, this *bunga* was demolished along with the others, with the intent of leaving no memory of great Sikh warriors. This remains an unknown fact for many of Panjab's youth today.

When the clock tower was finally brought down in 1945, a new *parikarma* was built. The bricks that once formed the *bungas* of inspirational Sikh warriors like Sada Kaur were once again found buried deep beneath the old ground. When those bricks were held close to the ear, it was as if they were echoing the names of *Sardar* Sher Singh, *Sardar* Ajit Singh, Sadarni Sada Kaur, and other beloved Sikhs of the Guru. The bricks were removed from the fires of oblivion into the cooling waters of the *Amrit*sar *Sarovar*. The bricks and mortar of this sacred place have seen many a turbulent time, but they have also paved the way for many great warriors, mystics, and enlightened souls. This is why they say to understand the true worth of Darbar Sahib, look not towards the gold that has been wrapped around Harmandir Sahib, but look instead towards the countless skulls laying beneath the *parikarma* upon whose sacrifices Sikhs today walk, have *darshan* of the *Amrit Sarovar* and listen to the soul-piercing melodies of the Guru's Bani.

Sada Kaur, too, was now living within the *parikarma* of Darbar Sahib, under the shelter of Guru Ram Das' sanctuary. She had built a small *bunga* a few years before, which had three floors. Whenever she had time to take a break from the worldly responsibilities of leading both the Kanaiya and Sukerchakia Misls, she would go there and spend some time in the Guru's *Sangat,* reflecting and meditating on *Akal Purakh* Vaheguru.

Following the disagreement over Vadni Fort, Maharaja Ranjit Singh had spoken to Sada Kaur in a manner that he should never have even thought of doing. Overcome with ego, he had forgotten the sacrifices and blessings Sada Kaur had bestowed upon Ranjit Singh for over forty years. When the time came to issue the order, he did not do so himself but sent Gulab Singh Dogra to issue the order. Upon hearing it from his mouth, Sada Kaur only spoke a few words, "I will not live in Lahore, nor will I stay in Batala. I will spend my final days in the sanctuary of Sri Darbar Sahib."

In an attempt to appease Sada Kaur, Gulab Singh had made some comments about the Maharaja. Such was Sada Kaur's character that, though her soul had been deeply hurt by his actions, she did not allow Gulab Singh to continue. She had immediately stopped him in his tracks and told him, "This is a family issue. You do not need to concern yourself with it. Just honour your role as the messenger and be on your way."

On the same day, Sada Kaur had also spent some time speaking with Sher Singh. He was still of the view that a revolt was needed; however, Sada Kaur explained the importance of a unified Panjab. Soon after this, Sada Kaur and two of her aides had left for *Amrit*sar.

Upon reaching Darbar Sahib, Sada Kaur first bowed in Harmandir Sahib, then she walked around the *parikarma* and did an *Ardas*, and then made her way over to her small *bunga.* As she began to unpack her belongings, Sada Kaur felt a strange separation. Even though she had stayed in this *bunga* many times before, on that day, everything appeared foreign, like her *haveli* in Batala had felt in her final days there.

In the past, Sada Kaur would spend her time reading and listening to *Gurbani*, doing *Simran*, and spending time amongst the Sangat that had travelled to Darbar Sahib. On this day, however, she was still in a state of heightened anxiety. The walls appeared dull, the ceiling looked gloomy, and in many ways, she felt it was a prison cell. Later that day, she went over to the *sarovar,* bathed, recited the sweet words of *Rehras Sahib*, and made her way back to the *bunga.*

When night fell, she sat on her bed and read *Sohila Sahib*. She then placed her head on the pillow and tried to get some rest. Taro and Tejo, her two servants, were with her in the *bunga*, resting in the room next door. In those days, upon the beds in the *bunga* there was a kind of netting dangling from the ceiling, in the middle of the bed. This netting was used to keep out mosquitos and the like during the night. Sada Kaur reached up and unravelled the netting, which sprung out to all four corners of the bed like a tent.

As the night passed, Sada Kaur struggled to sleep. Tossing and turning, she was wide awake in the middle of the night. Suddenly, she heard the cries of a young child. She sat up, rubbed her eyes and looked around the room, but could not see any child. There was a slight opening in the wall that looked over the *parikarma*, through which the moonlight shone into the room. Sada Kaur peered through the small opening but could not see any child. At first, she had thought it was one of her grandsons, but they, of course, were no longer children. Looking around the room, Sada Kaur said, "Is anyone there?"

After a few seconds, Taro came rushing into the room and said, "Yes, what can I do for you, Mata ji?"

"Where is the child who is crying?" asked Sada Kaur.

"There is no child, Mata ji; everyone is asleep. The *parikarma,* too, is quiet, with only a few Sikhs asleep under the arches. I didn't hear any cries; I have been awake," said Taro.

"That is strange; I can't sleep, but when I close my eyes, I hear the cries of a young child."

"It's not a dream is it, Mata ji?"

"Dreams occur when we sleep, Taro, I am awake."

"You're not worried about anything, are you, Mata ji?"

"No, no. I don't have any worries."

*"Mata ji, Satnam Vaheguru da jaap karke sonjo;"* Dear Mother, meditate on Satnam Vaheguru, and you'll slowly drift off to sleep.

Sada Kaur smiled and ushered Taro to leave. Upon Taro leaving the room, Sada Kaur heard the cries again. This time she jumped up, moved aside the netting, and stood up.

"O' Vaheguru, what is happening? There is no child in the room, but why can I hear the sound of a child's cry? My own grandsons are now older, I've accepted I have no son of my own, so why is my mind still playing these tricks?"

Sada Kaur walked over to the walls where her weapons were hanging. Looking at them, she thought about all the battles she had fought for over forty years. The scene of each battlefield appeared before her.

"I did not do this; I don't wish to fall prey to my ego. This was only possible with the strength and support of *Akal Purakh* Vaheguru. I can never raise a revolt against Ranjit, nor can I allow one to happen. My people have finally found some peace and stability after so many years of turmoil. There is no imminent threat of an *Abdali* or *Nadar*, and I do not wish to sabotage the current environment across Panjab where people are happy and building their lives."

Sada Kaur thought for a moment, then, walking back to the bed, she sat down and thought about her status across Panjab. She knew all of Panjab regarded her as a respected and wise woman; many referred to her as the mother of Panjab. Thinking about this, Sada Kaur spoke out again, "The disagreement regarding my Forts of Vadni and Himmatpur is my own personal issue. I cannot allow my own personal disagreements with Ranjit to boil over and adversely affect the entire country. I cannot allow Panjab to be split or forced to choose between Ranjit and me. The same Panjab for which I worked so hard to build is today full of vibrant flowers and fruit - why should I cut down and burn my own garden? O' Vaheguru, please bless me so that I may quieten this mind and rid myself of this worry."

Sada Kaur called for Taro and asked for a glass of water. After taking a few sips, she placed the glass down and headed back to bed. Taro watched as Sada Kaur mumbled some words until she eventually closed her eyes and fell asleep.

# 21.

Days turn to months, and months into years. A person thinks their time on earth greatens, but in reality, as the years pass, their time on earth diminishes. The end time approaches faster than many realise - no one can run from that final day. On the one hand, the soul, having become attached to the temporal pleasures of this world, tries to cling on to what it can, and on the other hand, the supreme-soul instructs *Dharamraj* to judge the actions of the soul once it leaves the cage of its body. People have called that moment of final departure the moment of death.

Those people who have spent their lives in service of others, bettering the world and challenging oppression - they have no fear of death. They have meditated on *Akal Purakh*, and they look forward to the day they merge back into the ultimate light. This is because death is the only certainty in life, and it is not something to fear - it is a complete truth. Their faces are not full of doubt, regret, or anxiety, but they radiate with the fullness of life and death.

It was December 1932, and Sada Kaur was now into her seventies. That month, and that year, would be her last on this earth. The messenger of death had departed, and Sada Kaur was unable to leave her bed. Her body had grown old and weary, her hair was all white, but her ever-radiant face could light up any room. While she was unable to move around, she recognised everyone that came in to see her. Beside her was a doctor, a *Granthi*, and her servants, but none of her own was with her at that time. Sada Kaur was cognizant of this reality, and it brought a new sadness. She had always thought her son, grandsons, and other family would be there with her during her last moments.

Sada Kaur thought, *are they that engrossed in worldly affairs that they cannot find a little time to visit me before I depart this earth? I can never forget my son, Ranjit Singh, grandsons Sher Singh and Tara Singh, and my daughter Mehtab Kaur, but they appear to have forgotten me.* Sada Kaur knew her daughter had already left this world before her, and she hoped Mehtab Kaur was eagerly awaiting her arrival in the next world.

"Taro, have we received any news from Lahore?" Sada Kaur asked her servant.

"No, Mata ji. Although we have sent two horses - have a little faith, they will arrive soon," said Taro.

Sada Kaur remembered the day those messengers from Gujranwala had arrived with the news that Maha Singh was taking his final breaths and had asked for her. She had dropped everything that instant and ridden straight to Gujranwala to be with Maha Singh, even though he wasn't family and had colluded to kill her husband. It was about taking a principled stand and doing the right thing.

"Yes, they must be coming … but ..." started Sada Kaur.

*"Vaheguru da dhian dharo Mata ji;"* focus on Vaheguru, dear Mother, said Taro.

"Vaheguru is the one calling me, dear; the messenger of death is at my door," replied Sada Kaur.

"Do not say such words."

"It is true, dear; I know my time is near."

"My Mehtab Kaur's beloved sons, Sher and Tara …?"

"Yes, Mata ji, they are on their way."

Sada Kaur nodded and closed her eyes. Night was falling over the cold days of December. Taro and Tejo lit some candles around the *bunga*. The flames flickered in front of Sada Kaur, and she softy said, "Another day has passed. No one will travel in this darkness now. Perhaps they are busy, or maybe they are engaged in a battle. I wish them all the best in maintaining the glory of *Khalsa Raj* over Panjab."

"Yes, Mata ji," said Taro.

"Taro, please call Keso. I want her to come and sit beside me."

Taro called for Keso. Keso was a bright young servant who Sada Kaur felt would go on to serve the Raj well. As she arrived, Sada Kaur asked her to sit beside her. Keso did that and began to massage Sada Kaur's feet.

"Tell me, Keso, is it true there are no imminent threats to the Lahore Darbar?" asked Sada Kaur.

"Yes, Mata ji. The Maharaja has solidified our Raj. The British stay beyond the Satluj and do not dare look towards Panjab while the Maharaja sits in Lahore. The sovereign flags of the Khalsa fly in Kashmir, Hazara, Haripur, Peshawar, Vazirstan, Multan, and Kangra."

"It is a very expansive Raj."

"Yes, Mata ji, all possible because of your efforts."

"I did nothing. It was all the work of *Akal Purakh* Vaheguru. I was but a woman."

"No, Mata ji, you are one of the most courageous and fearless women to have walked this earth. The whole of Panjab knows of your bravery ..."

Sada Kaur could not listen to her own praise, so interrupted Keso, "No, no! This was all *Akal Purakh* Vaheguru. Sing the praises of the Almighty under whose protection Panjab grew to become such a strong and successful region of the world. In fact, I want you to send some *Seva* from me towards *Guru ka Langar* tomorrow and also distribute shawls to those who need them in these cold months of the year. For Harmandir Sahib ..."

Sada Kaur had just said 'Harmandir Sahib' when two servants came running in, *"Maharaja ji aagai, Maharaja ji aagai."* The Maharaja has arrived, the Maharaja has arrived!

Sada Kaur turned her head towards the door. Maharaja Ranjit Singh, Nau-Nihaal Singh, Sher Singh, and Tara Singh all entered the room. There was a look of shame and concern on all their faces. Their eyes were tearful.

Maharaja Ranjit Singh had not seen Sada Kaur for approximately eight years. It was not that he did not find time or that he was engaged in battles to protect the *Khalsa Raj*. He had been duped by the deceitful ways of the Dogras, who had spread lies about Sada Kaur, which had caused the Maharaja to doubt and disown the woman who raised him like her own. His mind was full of anger and jealousy as the Dogras turned the Maharaja against Sada Kaur.

On the other hand, Sada Kaur had always wished the best for the Maharaja. Even though he had taken her estates and effectively banished her from any political activity, Sada Kaur continued to pray for the Maharaja's health and welfare. When Keso would inform Sada Kaur of the Maharaja's latest victories, overcome with joy she would offer them all gifts. She would send donations to Darbar Sahib and ask for prayers to be held in honour of the Maharaja's successes. Sada Kaur only wanted the Maharaja to succeed so that Panjab would stay strong.

Sada Kaur had to endure eight years of constant harassment from the Dogras, who were frantically trying to turn her against him. But she remained steadfast in her own faith that one day she would have an opportunity to speak to the Maharaja herself. Alas! He had finally come to his senses and, upon hearing news that Sada Kaur was in her final days, he had travelled with his sons to meet her and offer his sincere apologies for the way he had treated her. In those last moments, he realized that he was blinded by his own ego as the supreme ruler of Panjab and that he should never have said such harsh words or sent Sada Kaur away.

As he stood there in the *bunga* around Darbar Sahib, the Maharaja held his head in shame, and a tear rolled down from his right eye. He walked towards Sada Kaur and said, "Mata ji ... please forgive me," immediately placing his head at Sada Kaur's feet.

"I have made so many mistakes but sending you away has been my greatest sin. I now realise you only wished the best for me. However, I lost my way and banished the one person who loved me more than anyone else."

Nau-Nihaal Singh, Sher Singh, and Tara Singh followed their father and bowed at Sada Kaur's feet. The *bunga* fell silent; not a sound was heard until Sada Kaur looked up, "My son. I just wanted to see you. This is not the time to spend too much time talking. I just want to say, forget everything."

"Please forgive me. My mind is full of worry, and I am full of regret for the way I have treated you. Forgiveness! Please, Mata ji, I ask you for forgiveness. I am speaking to you now as your son, Ranjit, not as the Maharaja. The same Ranjit that you raised and nurtured, the same Ranjit that would always seek your advice before he became a Maharaja. Despite your love and prayers, I betrayed you. Of all people, Mata ji! I betrayed you, and now I stand before you, asking for forgiveness."

Sada Kaur smiled and said, "Son, I forgave you a long time ago. I know some forces worked to break our bond. While those words came out of your mouth, they were put in your ear by others. I forgave you then, son, and I forgive you now."

The Maharaja stood up and walked up to the top of the bed, and taking Sada Kaur's hands, he knelt beside her. His mind felt instant relief. He had bottled up so many emotions for so long, but those loving words of Sada Kaur had dispelled all his anxieties. One thought kept running through his mind, *I wish I'd done this sooner.* Time waits for no one, and no one can bring back lost time.

"I wish to say one thing to you, son."

"Say as many things to me as you wish, Mother, I deserve all of what you throw at me."

"A king's job is to ensure his people are happy. This duty takes priority over his own happiness and desires."

"Mata ji, there is so much happiness and success within my *Khalsa Raj*."

"Son, never assume *Khalsa Raj* belongs to you. This claim to sovereignty was bestowed upon us by Guru Nanak Dev ji. You must always keep faith in the Guru and *Akal Purakh*."

"Yes, Mata ji. I understand."

"Don't rely so much on those Dogra ministers – they are like snakes. After you, they will throw poison towards the sons that stand beside you."

"I will remain vigilant, Mata ji."

"You are over fifty yourself now. This is no longer an age to marry other women. You do not need to marry daughters of these Dogras to maintain your hold over Panjab. Those kings who have many wives also sow seeds for future divisions and wars of succession. Those *firanghis* who you enlisted into the Khalsa Army at the behest of the Dogras, they will betray the Khalsa when the big wars begin. After all, son, they are foreigners, merely here to work and send money back home. They are not sons of Panjab; they are not sons of Guru Gobind Singh. They do not have the best wishes of the Khalsa in mind like our brave Singhs and *Singhnia*. That day is not far when the *firanghi* will betray all treaties and invade Panjab."

"No, Mata ji. While I live, no one dares to even look towards Panjab. If they do, I will rip out their eyes. *Khalsa Raj* is immortal – it will stay as long as the sun rises in the east and sets in the west. I am sure of this. Mata ji, please do not worry about that. I am praying that you can recover and walk beside me again. I will show you how expansive our kingdom has become."

Sada Kaur smiled. She had said what she wanted to on the matter and left the rest to Vaheguru. The doctor, *Granthi*, and others who were stood in the room all shed tears of happiness. They too had felt the eight-year separation between Sada Kaur and the Maharaja.

They continued to talk for a little while longer, trying frantically to catch up with the time they had spent apart.

When the time came, they all left the room, hopeful of visiting again soon.

For them, that day never arrived. Sada Kaur's health deteriorated that night. In the early hours of the next morning, the doctor was called. Sada Kaur could not speak and was drifting in and out of consciousness as her soul moved between two worlds. When day broke, the sweet melodies of Sukhmani Sahib could be heard reverberating around the *parikarma* of Darbar Sahib. Little birds had appeared outside the *bunga* and started their morning songs. The mighty Sada Kaur, whose sword carved a beautiful new map of Panjab, breathed her last and departed this world.

## Glossary of Terms

*Akal Purakh* - The Timeless Being

*AL-Lat* - Arabian goddess of war and combat, known in Greek mythology as Athena.

*Amrit* - Nectar of Immortality, as prepared by Guru Gobind Singh in 1699

*Amrit Vela* - Ambrosial hours of dawn

*Ang Sang* - Forever near

*Antim Ardas* - Final Sikh supplication

*Ardas* - Sikh supplication

*Baba* - Grandfather, also used out of respect to address an elder male

*Bhatts* - Ballad singers

*Bir Asan* - Warrior's pose

*Bir Asan Bani* - Warrior's mantra, also used to refer to Guru Gobind Singh ji's *Dasam Granth* (writings).

*Budha Dal* - Senior Army, employed mainly for garrison duties requiring less mobility

*Bunga* - place of dwelling

*Chandi* – sword, also used as reference to Hindu goddess of war

*Chardikala* – Sikh doctrine of an ever-rising spirit

*Chola* – Traditional warrior dress

*Chuni* - Headscarf

*Dal Khalsa* – Army of the Khalsa

*Dasam Granth* – Guru Gobind Singh ji's writings

*Dastaar* – Turban

*Degh* – lit. Kettle used to refer to food prepared in communal kitchen

*Dharam* – Righteousness, also used as synonym for faith

*Dharamsala* – lit. A place to learn about the practice of a religion, also place of meditation

*Dharmic* – To be of a righteous nature

*Dharamraj* – One who judges our actions after death

*Divan Khana* – Political office

*Dumalla* – Turban worn by Khalsa warriors

*Fateh* – Victory, also a salutation for the Khalsa, as in Vaheguru ji ka Khalsa, Vaheguru ji ki Fateh

*Firanghi* - Foreigner, a term used for the British

*Granthi* - An individual learned in *Gurbani*

*Gurbani* - The Guru's Word

*Gurdwara* - lit. Doorway to the Guru, also used as name for Guru's House

*Gurmatta* - Political decision-making assembly of Sikhs

*Gurmukh* - One who obeys the Guru

*Gurmukhi* - Guru's script

*Haveli* - House

*Jatha* - Unit of Sikhs

*Jathedar* - Head of unit of Sikhs

*Ji* - Used as a show of respect, normally after addressing someone by name

*Jujharoo* - Sikh fighter

*Kabaddi* - Panjabi sport

*Kalgi* - Royal plume

*Kalgidhar Pita* - Guru Gobind Singh ji, the wearer of the plume

*Kamarkasa* - Cloth tied around waist during battle or service

*Kavishris* - Poets

*Khalsa* - Collective of initiated Sikhs

*Khalsa Raj* - Sikh political rule

*Kirpan* - Sacred sword

*Kurta* - Panjabi dress

*Langar* - Food from Guru's communal kitchen

*Mahal* - Royal palace

*Mala* - Rosary beads

*Mandir* - Hindu place of worship

*Manja* - Wooden bed

*Manmukh* - One who obeys their own mind, does not listen to the Guru's Word

*Mata – M*other, or simply a term used out of respect to address an elder female

*Maya* - Illusion or Duality

*Mela* - Festival

*Misl* - Military unit, also term used for territories acquired by the Sikhs

*Nagara/Nagaray* - Battle drum(s)

*Narsingha* - Battle horn

*Nawab* - Governor/officer of land

*Nishan Sahib* - Sikh flag

*Nitnem* - Daily recital for Sikhs

*Panj Pyar-e* - Five beloved Sikhs of the Guru

*Parikarma* - Pathway surrounding Harmandir Sahib in *Amrit*sar

*Patshah* - Sovereign

*Pentra* - Style of battle movement

*Phulkari* - Panjabi design

*Pita ji* - Father

*Ranjit Nagara* - a Sikh war drum

*Rehat* - Discipline

*Rehras Sahib* - Daily prayer for Sikhs normally reciting around sunset

*Sadhana* - Daily spiritual discipline

*Sadhu* - Saint

*Salvar* - Dress

*Sant-Sipahi* – Saint-Soldier

*Sarbat Da Bhalla* – Welfare for all, a key Sikh philosophy

*Sarkar* – Your highness/your majesty

*Sarovar* – Reservoir/tank of water

*Sati* – The act of a widow jumping into her husband's funeral pyre

*Shabad* – Guru's Word

*Shahzade* – Prince

*Shastar Vidhia* – Science of weaponry

*Shiv ji* – Hindu god

*Sikh Sardars* – Sikh Chief

*Simran* – Meditation

*Sindoor* – Small line or dot of red powder above the forehead, a sign of a wedded women

*Singhni(a)* – Daughter(s) of Guru Gobind Singh

*Sochi* – Panjabi sport

*Sohila Sahib* – Daily prayer for Sikhs normally reciting at night, before going to sleep

*Taruna Dal* – Junior Army

*Tegh* – Sword

*Tyar-bar-tyar* – Ever ready